MERRY ELFING CHRISTMAS

Ever Rose

To Wendy, you are missed more than you will ever know.

The most important thing is, even when we're apart ... I'll always be with you.

A. A. Milne, <u>Winnie-the-Pooh</u>

FREAKING ELF ON THE SHELF

Tucking Daisey into bed, I stare at that little freaky elf that she insisted on her daddy buying. Truth is that the freaking thing freaks me out. I mean, who the heck came out with this crap?

Isn't it enough that we have to pretend to be Santa and bake cookies that I have to shove in my mouth because mommy loves oatmeal raisin cookies and snickerdoodles? Only to have to run that crap off the next day after a long night of wrapping and setting out the gifts that I get no credit for. The long hours and extra shifts to see the smile on her face I get no freaking credit for.

Speaking of the dingleberry, he's calling me now. "Christopher," I answer.

"Delilah," he answers back in the same tone of irritation. His voice makes me want to smash everything in sight as I take the freaky elf that he got her and plan for their demise. "I wanted to get Daisey for Christmas."

I dreaded this call. I didn't want to miss Christmas with her, but it was, in fact, a part of our agreement that he gets her this year for Christmas. My chest buckled at the thought. "I know."

Even though I couldn't stand him, he was a wonderful dad. It's the only thing I can give him credit for in our relationship.

"I will pick her up from school on Friday and bring her back on Wednesday. We are going to Shane's this year."

"Hold on, Shane lives in Florida. What about Christmas Eve at your mom's?"

 For the past four years, we had always shared Christmas Eve at his mom's. Now he was getting Christmas and Christmas Eve. My blood boiled.
"Yeah, we all are going," he said matter-of-factly.
"You're taking my daughter out of state for Christmas." I swing the poor elf around by the neck, thinking of him.
 "I'm taking our daughter to my brother's. It's family and Christmas."

 I think he was missing the point while I put the freaking Elf and Elsa on the counter with her Barbie frozen in ice. I think Barney, the elf, has it out for Barbie at this point in my life. Thank you, Pinterest, for all the ideas.

The chances of this elf getting action were greater than mine.

"You can always tag along," he said. "Tag along?" With a sarcastic laugh, I questioned his sanity. "I rather jump off a bridge and take my chances." There's not a chance in hell I would go to Florida with them.
 I could barely stomach my time with Christopher, much less Christopher and Shane together for a few days.
 Not that I despise Shane. In fact, it's the exact opposite. Shane was my high school crush, that happened to be Christopher's older brother. "I'll pass."
 "The invitation is open. I know you don't want to miss Christmas with Daisey, and I'm sure Shane wouldn't mind."
 "Well, you're not giving me much of a choice," I say, writing a note from Barney. *Look what Elsa did.*

My adult version would say something different. Barbie is a skinny heifer who has everything, so I froze that bitch.

 "Just think about it."
Oh, I was going to think about how much I hated him for taking her away for Christmas. "Sure. Is that all you wanted?"
"Goodnight Delilah."
 "Bye." I hung up and throw the phone onto the counter, deciding this Christmas was about to suck, and shoved a snickerdoodle into my mouth.

"Momma, momma." Daisey awoke me yelling. "Elsa froze Barbie!" She pulled at my arm. "Come look."
My eyes rolled and my head banged from the bottle I drank after the phone call.

"Barney looks so sad. Doesn't he momma?"

"Yeah, sweetie, he does," agreeing with my yawn, only ten more days of this shit, but who's counting? Oh, that's right, five. That little freaky elf is going with her. I smile at that thought.

"Barney wants chocolate chip waffles for breakfast." She smiles and waves the elf around.

"He does, does he?"

"Yep, with extra whipped cream." She beams her beautiful smile at me. You know the one where your kid knows exactly how to get what they want, that one.

Christmas Cheer & Lots of Beer

"We are slammed." Jessica walked by with a tray of beer. She reminded me of Jessica Rabbit with her red hair pinned to the side and the elf hat. Her red slinky dress pushed her boobs up high and the slit that went up her mile-high legs. If I had a body like hers, I'm sure I would flaunt it, too.

I've been trying to drop the weight I gained after Daisey, but I've faced the fact my body just isn't ever going to be a size two again. My black leather shorts and red shirt were about as scantily clad as I've gotten in a while. My assets seemed to create bigger tips, and I had plenty of assets to show off.

It was the Christmas season with holiday parties and drunk people. Mostly douchebags and assholes that thought we were their serving wenches to serve any of their needs as the night went along. I didn't put up with that and our regular patrons knew that. "Table seven is all yours." Jessica walked by. "Don't forget your elf hat."

"Freaking elves. Whose idea was this shit?" Putting on the hat.

"Yours," she reminded me.

"I had to be drunk, high or something?" I could hear her laugh as I hit the silver swing door with my side and put on my bright fake smile for tonight.

Table seven held a party from one of the marketing offices down the block. They weren't usually a rowdy bunch, but by the fifth round of beers, my Christmas cheer was running thin. The three other smaller tables I served came and went with small tips because every two seconds, table seven was flagging me down.

"Ssugarpplum." Table seven waved me over. The guy wearing the Santa hat calling me was sloshed and slurring.

"Yes." My patience was wearing thin with the nickname they have given me.

"How bout another round? "He waved his hand in a circle in the air. "Sure thing." Turning around and he slapped my ass.

That was it, I had it. My Christmas cheer went right out the window, continuing to the bar. Taking the elf hat off, and put the mugs of beer on my tray.

"Oh, shit," Kelvin the bartender said, looking at me. "Don't do it."

"Me, I'm not going to do anything. One extra, please."

"Can't do that." He takes the white

bar towel and wipes the bar clean, giving that I know what you are thinking look.

"You're no fun tonight."

"If you planned to drink it." He cocks his head to me.

"Never mind." I prance my black stilettos over to the table and serve the round of drinks.

"What happened to your hat, Ssugarpplum?" His eyes roamed up and down me. "Why don't you come sit on Santa's lap? I'm sure you've been a naughty girl." His chair turn so I could sit as he patted his lap.

"How about I don't and you get to keep your balls?" My black stiletto heel missed his precious jewels, but I think he got the message.

"Damn Ssugarpplum, I was just playing." He held up his hands, and I hear Pete call my name.

"Fuck," I say, spinning around. I knew this wasn't going to be good sitting my tray on the bar and going through the silver swing door.

 "Dalilah, you can't treat our customers like that. Go home," Pete huffed.

"You're freaking firing me for that shit?" Putting my hand on my hip. "The dick had it coming."

"Regardless, you can't do that. I believe it was you that said it's just a bar."

My words and thoughts were correct. It was just a bar, after all. "Fine." Walking back to our lounge to gather my things.

"We both know you are meant to do bigger things," Pete said from behind me. He is a sweet man that was my father's friend. "It would piss your Pop off that you have stayed here this long."

He had to go and use my dad to make this feel okay.

"I know." Turning to him and hugging him. "Have a good Christmas."

You Should Go

I stare at the freaky elf sitting on the counter contemplating what Barney was going to do tonight. I was running out of ideas. He's already made Hersey poos on cookies, went on a date with Barbie, made a snow angel in my flour, blew a bubble gum bubble fart, burned her toast for breakfast, and toilet papered the tree.

Sipping my wine and scrolling through Pinterest again, a knock on my door interrupted me. Looking through the peephole, it was Jessica. "Hey." She stepped in when I opened my door. "I figured you'd want this." Handing me an envelope.

"What's this?"

 "Your tip table seven left you," she said with a smile.

"They left me a tip?"

"Yep, I didn't even split it with you. You earned that shit."

"It must be a dollar," I laugh and toss it to the countertop.

 "It sucks that he fired you." She collapsed onto my fire red couch that matched her outfit tonight.

"It's for the best. You want a glass?" Holding up the bottle.

"Nah, I've got a date with Mitchell."

"Mitchell, is he the one that has the massive schlong?"

"Yeah, that one." She smiled, and I shook my head. "Aren't you going to open the envelope?" Tapping her foot on the floor.

"If you insist, I know it's going to suck."

Opening the envelope, I blink. The wine must be making me see things.

"Four hundred, this was from table seven?"
"There's a note as well." She smiled.
I pulled out the paper. The apology was sweet and his number was at the bottom.
"If you think I'm calling him, you are insane."
"It's your choice, but he felt bad."
"As he should, for treating someone like that. I don't think I need someone like that around Daisey."
"No one said you had to have a serious relationship. Just get some. You are kind of wound tight these days."
"I'm not wound tight," I retort.
"If you say so." She batted her eyes.
 I shot her the middle finger.
"Well, maybe you should at least treat yourself to something. You deserve it, with all those extra shifts."

"Christopher is getting her for
Christmas Eve and Christmas. They
are going to see Shane in Florida."
 "Isn't Shane the hot brother?"
"Yeah. He invited me to go."
Collapsing onto the couch with her.
She laughed, "Now that sounds like a
way to spend Christmas."
"With Christopher, no thank you?"
"No. In Florida, sipping Pina Coladas
on a beach with a hot guy. You should
go."
"Are you insane?" Sipping more wine.
"You know you want to see Shane.
Maybe two can get your freak on for
the weekend and call it good."
"Shane isn't going to give me the time
of day. Especially after my drunken
mistake with his brother," I sigh. "But
Pina Coladas on the beach sounds
like the vacation I need."
"I would go if I were you. How bad
could it be? Well, I've gotta go.
Mitchell is on the way to my

apartment." She looks down at her phone and smiles.

 "Well, have fun riding him all night. While I have to figure out what to do with this freaking elf again." I swing him around and look at the ceiling fan. I smile.

 "Take that trip and find you a schlong to ride." She winked as she went to the door. "And get rid of the elf. It freaks me the fuck out."

"Thank you, this thing freaks me out too!" I laugh and sip my wine.

 After the fifth time of strapping the elf to the ceiling fan, it worked when I turned it on low. Next was Barbie and Barney's other friend's turn to get strapped in for their ride.

 After three days of thinking about the invitation to go to Florida, I made the call to Christopher. He was surprised and so was I that I was going along on the trip that could easily turn into a disaster with us in close quarters.

You Have to be Elfing Kidding Me

Hearing the horn, Daisey yells from the window. "They're here, they're here, momma."

"I can hear that." Trying to zip my suitcase. I may have packed one too many things. Just maybe.

 "Mom, come on!"

The horn beeps again. "Yeah, yeah, hold the fudgesicle on. Mommy is having issues." I had a lot of issues, one being to be trapped in a car with Christopher for the next ten hours, not including pit stops. Six hundred and fifty agonizing miles, but who's counting? That would be me.

 Opening the door, my eyes bug out of my head. "You have to be elfing kidding me."

Daisey swings the elf as she runs to her dad. "Whoa, this is cool!" I hear her say as I slam the door and lock it.

"One bag each, is that all?" Christopher asked, popping open the side of the black bus RV. I wasn't even sure what it was other than huge as fuck.

"Are you trying to compensate for something? Did we need this big thing to go to Florida? And yes, only one bag each." Looking at all the luggage in the undercarriage.

"I wish Rachel wasn't as high maintenance," he said under his breath.

"Rachel, your girlfriend?"

"Yes, my girlfriend. And this." He pointed. "This is Shane's idea. So maybe, yeah, he might be trying to compensate for something."

"Shane?" I question, sipping on my coffee.

"Someone call for me?" He questions.

 What coffee I had in my mouth came flying out. "You have to be fucking kidding me. Christopher, can I talk to you?"
 We walk to the side out of earshot of whatever it was we were taking this trip in. "What the hell? You could have told me that Rachel and Shane were coming with us."
"Don't forget mom," he added with a smile.
I could feel myself about to lose my shit as I walk off.

"Dalilah, nice to see you again." Shane smiles his million-dollar, making you want to drop your panties for him smile.
 This was about to be awkward. I would have to hold it together and watch my words since Rosie is with us.
 Smiling back. "Nice of you to get us this delightful ride." My tone was sarcastic stepping up into the bus. It

was fancy and decked out. It was like nothing I'd ever seen before. "Holy shit." I cover my mouth. "Sorry, Rosie."

"If that's the worse it gets during this trip, we will be just fine. Merry Christmas, honey." She hugs me.

"Momma, come look at this bed," Daisey yelled from the back. Rosie released me, only to be hugged by Rachel.

 "OMG. I'm so glad you came. This is going to be so much fun." She releases me. "We can have a girls' day, go shopping, and go to the spa." She bounces on her heels with excitement and her voice hit a high pitch that made me want to poke my eyes out and cut off my ears.

"Yay." My sarcastic tone.

"Momma, it's so bouncy."

"Stop jumping on the bed," I yell.

"She's fine," Rosie said with a smile. "Let her have some fun."

I roll my eyes as I walk to the back.
Going by the row of bunk beds,
knowing that would be my sleeping
quarters.
 "Stop, please. Go back up front."
"But grandma told me I could."
"I'm sure she did, but I've asked you
to stop." Giving her I'm the boss look
and she stopped.
"Fine."
 Her attitude she got honestly from
me and the fuck you look also
honestly from me. "This so wasn't a
good idea." I exhale and turn around.

"Let's get this show on the road,"
Shane said, sitting in the driver's seat.
 "More like a shit show. Mind if I sit
here?" Pointing at the tan seat beside
him and he laughs.
"Make yourself at home. I miss your
smart mouth."
"It's only gotten worse." Smiling over
to him, he said he missed me. I
swoon at the thought and move on.

"When was the last time we saw each other?" He asked. His eyes twinkle to me, making my insides flip flop.
"The last shit show, at Daisey's first birthday."
"Oh yeah. What the hell were you thinking?" He laughs.
"How I thought a family function celebrating her birthday possibly couldn't go wrong? Right about now, I'm thinking the same thing about this trip." I peer over to him, thinking this could either go very wrong or very right.
"Honesty. I like it."

"Momma, where's Barbie? Barney is missing her." Waving the elf in my face.
"She's in your bookbag." Pointing towards her bag in the living area.
"What's with the freaky elf?"
"Christopher got it for her. It's an Elf on the Shelf."
"What's that mean?"

"It's Santa's helper. He will tell Santa if you are naughty or nice. Parents make the elf do things every night."
"Like what?" He said, turning onto the interstate.
"Let's see." Tapping my finger to my temple.
"Last night he pooped peppermints into the toilet. He has toilet papered the Christmas tree. He's wrapped the toilet in Christmas paper a few nights before. You should look it up when you get time. There are some funny ones."
 "Momma, look at what Rachel got me." Holding up the box of makeup.
 "How nice," I say with a smile and she ran back to them.
 "Great, she's going to have my daughter looking like a slut before this is over."
I could hear him chuckle. "It's not fucking funny. She is five, not fifteen. There are some sick freaks out there."

"True," he agrees.

"What do you do in Florida?" Asking to keep me from losing my shit because she is way too young for that mess.

"Real estate. What do you do now?" He asked, reaching for his energy drink.

"Nothing. I got fired from Eddie's a few days ago." Looking down at my feet and wondering what he would say next.

"You were still at Eddie's."

 "Yeah. Not exactly my dream job," saying with shame. It wasn't my plan to ever be there at twenty-five.

 "What are your plans now? You wanted to sing, didn't you?"

 "Yeah. It was just a dream I had, and before I had Daisey."

"Who says you can't still have your dream?"

  "Being a mom changes things." I close my eyes as I hear them sing

Christmas songs. "This is going to be a long trip."

"I second that," he chuckles in agreement.

"Music?" He asked.

"Anything but Christmas music."

"Your wish is granted." As he pushes play.

I smile as Metallica comes across the speakers.

"Mom said turn that shit off. She's trying to nap," Christopher said, strutting up front.

"Driver picks the music and shotgun shuts his cakehole," Shane said with a smile to his brother.

"You watch Supernatural," I say.

"Hello, just turn that crap down," Christopher replied.

"How about I just move it to these speakers?" He moves the nob.

I sing to the songs and close my eyes to relax into the big chair, thinking about Pina Coladas on a beach. I

think about what other wishes Shane
could grant me as well.

Does He Not Tell You Anything?

 "Well, we made it to our first stop without killing each other," he said, pulling into the park.
 "Why are we at Brookgreen Gardens?" I have always wanted to come here, but just never made it this far.
 "It's a part of the trip. Mom wanted to come to the Night of a Thousand Candles."
"Did Christopher not tell you our plans?" He questioned me with a look.
"No, I assumed we were going to a beach in Florida," he chuckled. "I hate to burst your bubble. Once we leave here, we're going to Disney."
"What the fudge?" Of course, he would plan something like this and

not tell me. "I guess I wasted the money I spent on that bathing suit. God, I was looking forward to sipping a Pina Colada on the beach and meeting a hot guy." I leaned back into the chair with disappointment. "Just like him to screw with my hopes and dreams."

 Walking through the garden, I watched Daisey enjoy the lights with Christopher and Rachel. Walking far behind at my own pace, I wasn't alone as Shane stayed quietly beside me. He offered to take a photo or two of me in spots that I liked. Neither of us said much other than how pretty the lights were.

 "Why didn't it work out with you two?" He finally asked.

 "You know your brother, right? Although he's changed since he's met Rachel, for the good. He's a great father and we manage to co-parent well. We just aren't a match, I guess."

"What do you think of Rachel?" His look said a lot because I obviously have an opinion of her.
"She's good with Daisey despite her lack of mothering skills, but she's learning."
"What would you think if they got married?"
"I'd be happy, if they are happy." That was the truth.
"What would you say if he was going to ask her on this trip?"
"To marry him?" I stop in my tracks.
"Yeah."
"I guess I would be happy for them." Hoping that he wouldn't be asking soon.
"That's good."
"Why?"
"Because at the next set of lights he's going to ask her?"
"This trip just keeps getting better." I walk off with his answer, stewing in what was about to happen.

As we slowly walk together again, I hear a squeal. "I guess she said yes." I roll my eyes. Was I jealous that he had found someone? Maybe just a hint. It wasn't like I ever was in love with him. I just wanted someone to share my life with.

As we made it closer, Rachel ran to me. "We're engaged!" She hugged me, bouncing on her heels. "Isn't it beautiful?" She held out her hand.

"Congratulations." I tried to sound happy as I could.

Shane congratulated his brother with a pat on the back and we all gather to celebrate with hot chocolate. I was truly happy for them. I just wish I would have had more of a heads up. Our relationship, I wouldn't consider even a friendship, but this affects Daisey.

Our walk continues through the beautiful works of art and sculptures. The lights twinkled, and it was truly a

magical place with all the lights.
 "What's one of your Christmas wishes?" Shane asked.
I could say that I didn't accept this offer but part of me is enjoying it. Mostly I'm enjoying the conversation with him. "A white Christmas. I've never had one."
"Well, that is highly unlikely in Florida."
"You think." I smile with my sarcastic tone. "What would be yours?"
 "Having my family here is my wish. It was hard putting this together. I haven't seen them in three years."
"Wow, I didn't realize it had been that long."
 "Moving to Florida, I started my business, but I didn't realize all the other things I was missing.

"Daisey, go take a shower and get ready for bed," I say, sipping on the champagne Rosie got to celebrate the engagement.
 "Grandma, can I use the shower in your room?" She smiles that I'm going to get what I want smile.
"Of course you can," she agrees, as any grandmother would.
"Come on, I will help you," I said, taking her hand.
 After a few moments, I figured out how to work the shower. I wanted to use this shower later. The extra jets that had different settings to massage you looked like it would feel good. "Don't use all the hot water. Your clothes are on Grandma's bed."
"Okay."
 She started singing when I walked out.

Walking back outside to enjoy the rest of my champagne. Rachel was chatting up about wedding plans already while I tuned her out, mostly while scrolling Pinterest for elf ideas. Finding one for tonight finally and noticing that Daisey hadn't made it back out.

 "I better go check on Daisey," I say to Rachel. "No one will get a hot shower if I don't."

Shit, that champagne went to my head. Walking through the bus, my head started spinning.

Opening the door to the room, yelling at Daisey, "Other people do have to take a shower tonight, sweetie. Oh my God, I'm sorry." I cover my eyes and turn around. " I thought Daisey was still in here."

"She's asleep in the third top bunk, we played fort."

 "Okay, sorry again." Closing the bedroom door. Leaning against it and

I can for sure tell you he wasn't compensating for anything.

 I couldn't get it out of my head while I found what I needed for the freaky elf. Taking the shot glasses and fill them up with lemonade. I write a sign that said *Lemonade 25¢.*
 "What are you doing?" Shane said behind me.
"Elf shit."
"What's he doing with lemonade?"
"Watch and learn." I smile, finding the elf in her stack of toys. Leaning the elf against the wall like he was taking a piss into the next cup.

 He started laughing. "That's funny as shit. Wrong but funny."
"Thank you, I try my best." Looking at him, my eyes divert themselves down. *Sweet baby Jesus Stop trying to look, he's going to notice.*
"You played fort with her?"

"She didn't like the enclosed bunk
too much, so I acted like it was a fort.
I made it fun for her."
 "Thanks. You didn't have to do that."
"I know. It was fun acting like a kid
for a few minutes." He smiled.
"It can be."

 Everyone started walking back into
the bus to settle in for the night.
"Goodnight everyone," Rosie said,
walking to the back.
"I'm going to take a shower, you
joining," Rachel said to Christopher.
 I roll my eyes because of her
announcement. Some things other
people don't want to know.
Not that moments later we didn't
hear them.
"Kill me now." I plugged my ears.
"Music?" He said.
"God, yes, please."
"That's what she said." His smile
knowing and huge.

"That's not even funny." I shake my head at him and his joke. He turned on the music upfront to low to not bother everyone else.

"I'm sorry about walking in on you." Taking the last of my champagne in one gulp to deal with the noises and the schlong that I now can't get out of my head and his fucking gray sweatpants he had on. Does he not realize what women do when a man has gray sweats on? It's like porn for us.

Gray Sweats, Coffee, & Weddings

The smell of bacon and coffee permeated throughout the bus. Peeking up to see if Daisey was still sleeping, she wasn't in her bunk. I was sure it was Rosie cooking, but surprised when walking closer, I stop and listen to Mr. Gray Sweats and my daughter cooking. He had her in a chair helping. I couldn't help but to smile at the scene.

 "Momma likes it extra crispy. This isn't crispy enough."
"If you keep taste testing, no one else is getting bacon."
"And I like extra cheesy grits."
"Yes, boss," he laughed.

My heart melted, wishing her father
was more like his brother. I watched
for a moment longer before making
myself known.

"What are you two doing in here?"
"What does it look like, momma?
We are cooking, duh."
"Smells good," I say, making my
coffee.
"You know how I like my bacon."
"Crispy. He's working on it, momma.
I'll make sure he gets it right. I told
him if he didn't do it right, you would
spank him."
This was the second time I spewed
coffee in two days.
"That sounds promising." He looked
at me and I hit his arm.
"You're turning red."
"It's the coffee."
"Momma says you are never too old
to get a spanking."
"Jesus, go play. I think Barney was

looking for Barbie. Why don't you help him find her?"

"Okey-dokey." She hopped off the chair. "Momma, I wouldn't drink that lemonade." Pointing at the cups with her tiny finger.

"I won't." I giggle at my daughter.

"She's definitely your daughter." His eyes seemed to have a twinkle in them this morning.

"Yep." Sipping my coffee, I smile because she is truly a mini-me.

"How'd you sleep?" He asked.

"I had to put in my earbuds and listen to music to drown out Christopher's snoring."

"It was loud, wasn't it?"

"Like a fucking freight train."

"What's our plans today?"

"Getting spanked." He smiled.

"You're turning red again. This is fun."

"You can go spank yourself."

"Crispy bacon." He turned with a

plate. "I will later trust me." He winked. "You're red again."

"What's going on in here?" Rosie asked.
"Shane was just telling me that he was going to go spank himself later." He coughed.
"You okay." I patted his back.
"Yep. It's the bacon."
"Sure it is. Two can play that game."

"At least he wasn't like Christopher. He could never keep his hands off himself. I thought I was going to have to take him to a psychiatrist or something," Rosie explained, fixing her coffee, with her rose-pink robe on and curlers in her hair.
"Well, that explains a lot," I say, sitting down.
"Mom, I don't think Christopher wanted you to tell people about that."

"About what?" He walked in, scratching himself and yawning. We both burst out laughing.
"What's so funny?"
"Nothing," we say in unison.

"Did he get it crispy enough, momma?" Daisey asked, sitting beside me.
"Yes, he did a good job."
"Your extra cheesy grits, madam." He sat her bowl down.
"This one can cook momma and he can follow directions."
She tried to whisper, but everyone heard. Was my daughter trying to play matchmaker?
"I'm going to get dressed. Eat your grits."

It wasn't long before we were on our way to our next destination, Florida. I made myself comfortable in the front again beside Shane and Daisey, spent time with her future stepmother planning a wedding and talking about dresses. I'm not a prissy girl, but I could pull it off when needed. Maybe it was a good thing she would have that with Rachel, or maybe not. I haven't figured that out yet.

"Dalilah," Rachel called.

"Yeah," I say, when she approaches us.

"How about this for your dress?" She put her phone in my face.

"My dress?" I asked, looking at the lavender dress.

"Will you be a bridesmaid?"

"Me? I couldn't." *Well, that just got weird.*

"You will. You can't say no to a bride."

Like hell, I couldn't. She looked at me with those eyes. She had that pouting thing down. I must give the chick credit. "Fine."

"Yay!" She jumped up.

"Yay." My tone was sarcastic as always, and Shane smiled. I wanted to flip him off. Instead, I gave him a half smile and an eye roll to let him know how I felt.

"We already have a date," she said. "I did some research last night." She grinned. "I hope you all don't mind, but we're doing it at the resort on Monday."

"You're getting married on Christmas?" I question her. "Like in three days?"

"Yep, isn't this exciting?"

"Oh, yeah. So exciting." I look at Shane and he shrugs his shoulders at me.

This trip just keeps getting better.

Are We There Yet?

"Momma, come look at what
happened to Barney!"
I hadn't done anything with Barney,
which freaked me out until I walked
into Rosie's room and laughed.
Barbie and Moana had taped him to
the wall. The sign read, *Barney must
choose one of us or else.*
"When did you do that?" Asking,
sitting back in my chair.
"Do what?" He smirked. "What? I
figured Moana needed to know, so
he's got what's coming to him."
"There's more?"
He grinned as he continued to drive.
It had me wondering what he's going

to do next. Thank God someone else was taking over the freaky elf.

I was humming in deep thought, smelling my marker doing my word puzzle when I heard Rachel call my name to come to look at some things.

"Oh joy, wedding shit." I cringe with unbridled joy.

"It can't be that bad."

"You didn't see the last dress she picked out for me. I shall return if I don't jump out the back window first." Unbuckling the belt, walking down what felt like death row to her. Her cheery, perky smile made me want to throw up.

"OMG, I found the perfect dresses for you and Daisey. They have them at a boutique near where we are staying. And in the right sizes. What do you think?"

I couldn't believe I kind of liked them. The burgundy dresses were alike and sweet looking. At least it wouldn't

look like I took a dip in Pepto-Bismol,
like the last one.

"I like them."

"Yay!" She clapped her hands in joy.

"I will call her back and have her hold
them."

"How much are they?" Asking, my
funds were tight because of
Christmas. I only had a few hundred
in mad cash after my shopping spree
with Jessica for beach attire I'm not
going to use.

"Don't worry about it, I got it." She
waved at me.

"No, Rachel, I can't let you do that."

"You will." She smiled that smile.

"You can't say no to the bride. Please,
no one expected this to happen on
this trip."

"Fine," I say through cringed teeth. I
hate taking what felt like a handout. I
worked hard for things and didn't like
it when people wanted to give me
things.

"What do you think about this one?"
She handed me her phone.
 "It's beautiful." The wedding dress
was beautiful and had to cost some
serious cash.
 Rachel's family had money, and she
was going to use it. I know I could talk
trash about how she can blow it, but
she works when she doesn't have to.
I have to give her credit from what I
know she's worked hard climbing the
ladder at the marketing firm she
works for.
"You think he will like it?"
She asked with an unsure smile.
"Yes. I'm going to fix a glass of wine.
You want some?" Asking her. I
needed to drown my feelings in
alcohol.
"Nah."
"You sure?" I knew Rachel was a
drinker. I've seen her get wasted
plenty of times at Eddie's.

"Yeah. I'm good." She smiled.
"More for me then." Fixing my glass.

 I sit on the couch with Daisey and start watching The Christmas Story with her and Rosie. I wasn't watching it much by the time I finished my glass.
Daisey had fallen asleep on my lap as I gently move so I don't wake her.

 "You're in my seat," I say to Christopher.
"I didn't realize we had assigned seating." He looked at me.
"Move." I put my hand on my hip.
"Say please." He smiled.
"How about getting the fuck out of my seat?" I grinned back at him.
"Hey, you two chill," Shane said. "Bro, just get up."
"Fine, here's your seat."
"Thank you." Giving him my eat shit grin.

"I thought I was going to have to send a search party," he said as I sat back in the passenger seat.

"Do you think Rachel is pregnant?" I ask him quietly.

"Do you?" Turning his head to look at me.

"Let's just say Rachel can party hard and she didn't even drink her champagne last night, and when I offered her wine, she declined." I arched my brow.

"Anything is possible, "he replied. "They obviously aren't practicing abstinence."

"This could explain why she wanted to have the wedding now." I go back to my puzzle until I get stuck on a clue.

"Are we there yet?" Asking him and humming to the song.

"Christopher wanted to stop before we get too close and give Daisey

something."
"What?" I ask because I've seemed to be left out of the loop.
"I'm not sure, other than it's letting her know we're going to Disney."
"How is he affording Disney?" I go back to my puzzle to figure out the next word.
"He can't. I have connections. Perks of the business."
"Was this whole trip your idea?"
"Pretty much."
I thought for a moment. Well, the wine seemed to be doing my thinking. "Did Christopher invite me on this trip?"
"He asked you, didn't he? This is our exit. You should go wake her up."
"I'll go wake her, but don't think that I didn't realize that you deflected."
Getting up and leaning to his ear. "I'm on to you, Shane Derby."

Maybe, just maybe, what I thought was left behind, once his brother so graciously knocked me up, wasn't.

You Have arrived at Your Destination

The bottle of wine that was in the fridge was sounding good as Daisey continues to list all the things she wanted to do at Disney. "Momma, who's your favorite princess?"
"That's a hard one, but it's probably Jasmine."
There were several reasons and none of them had to do with the movie other than the song.
"I thought it would be Cinderella," Christopher said behind me. "You seem more like a Cinderella."
I wasn't sure if that was a compliment or not.

"No, she's a Jasmine." Shane walked by. "Everyone ready."

"Yes! Get me to my destination, driver," Daisey directed.

"Yes, Madam. Your wish is granted."

"Why don't you go play with the new dolls that you got in grandma's room?"

She ran to the room as I lean back on the couch. This trip was draining the life out of me. Christopher gave her the best gift she's ever received, and it made me feel bad. I should have just stayed home.

I walk back to my seat up front because the couple that's smooching beside me is making me feel awkward and lonely.

"Only an hour left," he said as I sit down and looked at me. "What's wrong?"

"I work so fucking hard to give her a good Christmas and get no credit and he." I point to the back. "Gets to be super dad."

"A fucking trip to Disney."

"That he didn't pay for," he replied.

"She doesn't know that. I mean, he could have maybe said it's from all of us."

"Self-centered asshole."

"Dalilah. Christopher knows how hard you work to provide for her. He tells me all the time. He doesn't know how you do it."

"Yeah, I'm sure that's what he said."

"Seriously, he does." He tried to reassure me. "So don't think he doesn't see it. When he asked me, I wasn't sure if I should do this for him because we both know how he can be. I'm glad I did. I don't think this trip is all about him."

"Well, he sure seems to like the spotlight so far."

"Momma, have you seen Barney?" Daisey asked.
"No." Thank God.
"Look in Grandma's bathroom," Shane said. "I think I saw him in there.
"Okay." Her feet pitter-pattered on the floor to the back.
"What did you do?"
"Go see." He smiled.

"Honey, why don't you go see if daddy wants any of these Oreos that Barney made."
I handed her the bag and walked back up front.
"That was good. But you have to listen as I turn down the music so he could hear looking towards them.

"Daddy, try the Oreos that Barney made."
"No, why would you do that?" Shane said.

"Because it's going to be funny."
"You're naughty. Santa's not going to
bring you anything," he cautioned.
"I'll live," I say with a big smile as
Christopher takes one and pops it in
his mouth.
"What the fuck?"
"Daddy, watch your words,"
she said as he was spitting it out.
"I'm glad I didn't get his lemonade.
What is this?"
"He put grandma's toothpaste in
them," she laughed.

"Now that, my dear, was payback for
buying the fucking freaky elf."
I smile and continued my puzzle.
"What's another word for a come-
hither look?" I tap my marker and
hum to the music.
"Who the fuck has a come-hither
look, anyway?"
"Seductive," he replied.
I put the letters into the boxes.

"Thanks."
"Folks, our destination is on the right."
"Halle- freaking -lujah!"

"Dalilah, I have an appointment set for us at four to go get the dresses and the guys to go get their stuff."
"Rachel, can we get me a Belle dress?"
"Honey, we aren't doing Disney Princess dresses for the wedding, but we will see what we can find you for later." Rachel smiles at her.
Jesus, she is going to spoil my child rotten. Something about that made me smile.
It's not that I don't like Rachel, it's just that we are so opposite. She's all smiles and I'm... well, me.
It's not that I wasn't happy. It's just that luck hasn't been on my side lately. I think I've smiled more on this trip than I have all year. Shane has

always made me smile. That's the thing with him. He gets me. Nowadays I'm cautious with my love life because of Daisey. I don't want to bring someone into her life that isn't in it for the long term.

"Momma, don't forget Barney," she yelled as I picked up her things and packed them. She was busy chatting up Rachel about princesses.

"Here's everyone's keys to their suites." He handed Rosie hers and the blissful couple theirs.
"I think you forgot one?" I had my hand out.
"Did I?" He looked at me.
"Yeah, you did," I snarkily say back with my hand on my hip.
"Well, I will just have to fix that." He winked and walked off the bus with the others.

I huffed and wondered why I did this to myself. Oh, I thought I was getting a sunny beach while sipping on some drinks, working on a tan, and maybe a man. No, I got Disney and a wedding.

Connecting Rooms, Princesses Unite

"Stop jumping on the bed."
"It's so bouncy and fluffy, momma. I can't help myself." She bounced one more time.
The massive room had a king-size bed and the jacuzzi tub was calling my name tonight after being stuck in that bus for almost two days.
 "Momma, momma come look."
I look at the window at a pool.
 "Can we go swimming?"
"Maybe later we have to go get our dresses."
"What's that noise?" She asked.
"Someone's knocking on a door."
It wasn't coming from the entrance.
"Who's there?" The knock coming from a door in the kitchen area.

"It's Shane. Open up."
I unlock the door to his smile.
"We have conjoining rooms,"
he said.
"Oh, joy." Leaving the door open and
he walked in.
"What do you think?"
"I've been to nicer places." My tone
was sarcastic.
"Liar."
"It's really too nice. Thank you."
"I've come to get you two so we can
go meet up with everyone else."
"Not back on that bus," I pout.
"Your chariot awaits," he teased.
"I forgot something. I'll be right
back," he said as we were waiting on
the elevator.
"Go ahead down to the lobby if it
gets here before I'm back." He jogged
backward.
"He's funny. I like him," Daisey said. I
agreed with a nod.
Moments later, the elevator opened,

and he hadn't returned, so we got on the elevator.

"Did you forget something or get lost?"
"Good things come to those who wait," he teased.
"Tell that to a five-year-old. She will disagree with you, but good thing she went with her grandma. Rachel got the concierge to get them a car, so I guess it's just us."
"Well, I guess Daisey is going to be upset." We stopped after walking out the door.
"Mr. Derby," a man asked and handed him a key.
"Your chariot awaits." He opens the door to the white convertible for me.
 "Thank you. You are right, she would love this."
I enjoyed the top down and the late afternoon sun on my face.

When I walk in, Daisey already has
her dress on. "Momma, don't I look
like a princess?"
"Yes, baby, you do."
"I'm princess Daisey. You have to try
on yours, momma. So you can be a
princess too!"

"Are you all ready to see her dress?"
The shop owner asked us all while we
waited in anticipation.
"Yay!" Daisey jumped up and down.
When Rachel walked out, it brought
me to tears when Rosie started
crying. I normally didn't get
emotional about these things, but
she was stunning in the dress. We all
agreed that it was the one.

I looked around on the other side of
the boutique and found a cute dress.

Looking at the price, I put it back.
"You should get it." Rachel walked
over to me. "You could rock that."
"I shouldn't. I know Daisey is going to
want a lot of things in the park."
"Spoil yourself some. You've been
working hard lately. You deserve it."
I already felt bad for spending money
on myself for this trip, but I liked this
dress.
"I'll pass. I'm more of a jeans and tee
girl, anyway."

Daisey wouldn't stop chatting with
Shane on the way home about our
dresses and being a princess.
Their banter was comical as I enjoyed
the setting sun and the wind blowing
in my hair.

Opening the room door, Shane
stopped me from entering. His touch
lingering longer than it should have

as our eyes connected. Daisey yelled,
bringing my attention back to her.
"Momma, poor Barney. Come look."
"So this is what you were up to," I say
quietly, entering.
They taped Barney to the sliding door
and all the princesses stood looking
at him. The sign said, *Princesses
united girl power. Barney must go.*
"Shane, can you get Barney? I don't
want him to get hurt."
"Sure, kid." He smiled at her.

"Can we go to the pool?"
Daisey bounced on the bed.
"Sure." She needed to get some of
her energy out so I can go to sleep at
a decent hour.
Shane accompanied us to the pool
area and Daisey was disappointed
when we got down there and it was
closed for maintenance for the day.
"Well, now what?" I ask my new
partner in elf crime.

"I have an idea. It's just down the block."
"Let me get her out of her suit."
"No, I want to be a mermaid."
She gave me those eyes. The ones I couldn't ever say no to.
The mermaid suit didn't look like a bathing suit, it looked more like a Halloween costume. I'm sure people are used to seeing kids in all kinds of things around here.
I was glad I put on my Maxie dress as a cover-up.
"Okay. Let's go."
"Disney karaoke, really." I look at him. Daggers were shooting out, I was sure.
"She will love it," he said.
"Are you all like besties now?"
He shrugged his shoulders, and she pulled him in the door.
This trip turning out to be one I will never forget.

Disney Karaoke

How many times can I listen to the theme songs of Moana and Frozen before I needed a drink? Seven, it took seven. How many drinks did it take before they had me up on the stage? One and a half. Daisey's song choice was from Zootopia. We both loved this song. I could see her smile and dance around as I sang.
"Can I go up, mom?" She asked when I got back to the table.
"Aren't you tired yet?"
"Nope." She popped her p.
"Shane said I could." They both smiled.
Giving my eat shit smile to him and sipped on my Bahama Mama.
I was having fun other than the next kid also sang *Let it Go*.

"Just nothing from Frozen or Moana."
"Deal," they said together.
They left me at the table with my Bahama Mama as they sang Hakuna Matata. I tapped my foot on the floor and smiled. I forgot how good Shane could sing. We were in drama together, so we acted and sang together before. That's where my crush had started on a stage with us singing *Summer Nights* from Grease. I didn't get the part, and he did. It would have been nice to be Sandy. Instead, I was just a person in the background.
"How was I, momma?" Daisey pounced back up in her chair.
"Really, really, good." I smile at my mini-me.
"I think you two should sing *A Whole New World*." There's that I'm going to get what I want smile.
"You do, do you?"
"Yeah, I think he could pull it off. He's

super cute, don't you think,
momma?"
I'm not sure if my daughter is five or
fifteen sometimes, but I didn't
answer her question aloud. I had
always thought he was cute, but now
that's not how I would say it. It wasn't
just looks, it was everything about
him that made him attractive to me.
He was an all-around good person.
Which made me more attracted to
him than I had ever been.
"Come on." He pulled me away from
my Bahama Mama.
"Someone has to stay with Daisey," I
say.
"Come on Daisey," he said.
"If I know you, she knows this song.
We'll just sing it all together."
"Do you still know the words?" I ask
him.
"I guess we'll see," he said as the
music started.
I got lost in the song and his eyes

during certain parts. I felt like we were back in high school until Daisey took over the song.

He made subtle touches on my skin that lingered after his fingers left. He affected me and I wasn't sure how to handle it.

"Excuse me, Ms." A man walked up to me in the line at the bar. I was going to ignore him, but something told me not to.

"Yes." I smiled.

"I'm Michael Martin. I'm a talent scout. I couldn't help but listen to your performance earlier. I was here scouting for kids for a TV show, but I have a spot in an animated musical I think you would be good in. Have you ever done voiceover work?"

I couldn't help but let out a small laugh. "No."

"I think you have talent. Here's my card with my site on it. Think about it."

"Thank you." Taking the card from his hand, and examined it before walking back.

"I thought you were getting another drink?" Shane asked when I return empty-handed.

"Changed my mind." Flipping it over in between my fingers like a magic trick, listening to half the people butcher these Disney songs in good fun.

"What's that?" Shane asked.

"Some talent scout guy gave me his card. You wouldn't have anything to do with that?"

He looked at me like I had two heads. "What?"

"Nothing." I wave him off. I was unsettled. I didn't want to say what I was thinking because it would spoil the fun for Daisey.

"Can we do that again?" Daisey asked.

"We should bring Dad and Rachel."
"I don't know if we have the time."
"Aww," she pouted.
"Aren't you excited about tomorrow?"
"Yeah, I wish you would come?"
"It's just you, your dad, and Ms. Rachel," I say through gritted teeth.

Recalling my earlier conversation with Christopher, he said he felt like it needed to be just them. He wanted to do something special with her this Christmas before... It wasn't just them anymore.
"Holy shit," saying at my conclusion. I was right. I had to be right.
"What?" He asked.
"Nothing." It wasn't my secret to tell if I was right. Earlier I was just speculating, but that conversation all but confirmed it looking back.

"Gross momma, come look at what
Barney is doing?"
I walk into Shane's room to see
Barney using his toothbrush to wash
his butt with. I crack a small smile,
but I just wasn't in the mood tonight.
"Go take your bath. It's ready,"
I say to her.
"Can you turn on the jets?"
"No, that's for grown-ups."
"Fine."
She stumped off and I roll my eyes.

"Hey, what's up with you?"
Shane asked, noticing my mood.
"Did you have something to do with
that talent scout?"
"Why would you think that?"
"You have connections."
"Sure, but not that kind of
connection."
"I swear if you are lying to me."
I point at him.
"That wasn't me. How about helping

me set this up?" He pulled out a roll of bubble wrap.

"What are we doing? "

"The floor is bubble lava."

We roll out all the bubble wrap from the door to his bed and made a plan.

We sat on the couch watching a cheesy Christmas movie, waiting for her. "How long does it take her in the bath?"

"That tub is like a pool to her. There's no telling. I'll see if she is ready to get out yet?"

"It's time to get out."

"I'm not finished." She swam around with her dolls.

I pushed the button to let the water out. "Time to get out," using my mom tone, holding up a towel.

Walking out of the room, she was dressed and ready for bed, knowing

the next few minutes were going to
be full of loud pops and jumping.

"I guess I better be going." Shane
stood up from the gray couch. "Do
you want to say goodnight to
Barney?"
"Yeah." She followed him to the door
"Well, let's go see him." He opened
the door in the kitchen.
She laughed at the first hop she made
and the pops continued as they
hopped together popping.
 "Come on, momma, it's fun," she
laughed.
"Come have some fun." He held out
his hand to me. "Pretend it's
Christopher."
I crack a smile and jump on one with
a loud pop. I continued hopping
around and laughing.
Our bodies connected when we
jumped to the same place. I jumped
back, removing myself from the

electricity that pulsed between us. It scared me. He scared me. It was written all over my face as he stepped closer to me with intention. I stepped back again.

"Momma, I found one more." She hopped, and it popped. "This is fun," she claimed.

"I think it's time to go to bed," I said, with my eyes still connected to his.

"But I'm having fun."

"It's late and you have to rest for tomorrow. Don't you want to be able to ride all the rides?" Breaking my stare and looking at her, seeing the disappointment on her face.

 "I guess." She walked towards the door.

"Tell Barney goodnight."

 She walked to the freaky elf and hugged it. Then she did something I didn't expect her to do.

"Goodnight Shane, I had a super fun

night." She hugged him and he hugged her back.

"I had a super fun night, too."

She released him and went into the room. I heard the bounce on the bed.

"I better make sure she goes to sleep. Goodnight."

"Goodnight." Closing the door behind me.

Pool Side Service

Even after soaking in the tub relaxing my body, it was my mind that had me staring at the ceiling. I got up and lightly tapped on the door, hoping he wouldn't answer. After waiting for a moment he didn't, I walked to the minibar, grabbed the cookies from it, and sat on the chair.

Why was I having these thoughts about someone that I know it wouldn't work with? He's in Florida and I'm three states away. I have a child with his brother. That's a good way to mess with your child's head. Family functions would sure be awkward. Thinking about things, I stuff the chocolate chip cookies into my mouth. Deciding that stuffing my feelings away would be the best thing to do.

"Be good and listen to them." I hug my baby.
"Make sure she stays with you. And not too much junk food." Looking at Christopher.
"I think I know how to take care of her."
"Well, this is a big playground for her. She can be a lot sometimes."
"You listen to your dad and Rachel," I tell her again.
"Yes, ma'am."
I watch them walk out the door and my heart sinks.
Falling onto the couch, I put on a cheesy Christmas movie. Two knocks on the conjoining door, I yell, "Come in!"
"What's your plans today?"

I shrug my shoulders. "I guess just chill and watch horrible Christmas movies."

"I'm going to the pool if you want to join."

"I don't know. I think I'm just going to stay in here for a while."

"This is Florida. You can't stay in your room when it's sunny and warm out. I know it's not a beach, but you never know."

"Nah."

"Get your suit on and come on. I believe it was you that wanted to sip on Pina Coladas with a hot guy. I can provide both." He smiled that you know I'm right smile.

"So you are going to find me a hot guy?"

"What, I'm not hot enough for you?" He was exactly hot enough for me.

"I've seen hotter." I let my eyes roam him.

"Cabana seven, if you change your mind."

I swear if this hotel phone rings again, I'm going to throw it off the balcony. I sit back down to watch the movie where she meets a prince during her trip to Ireland for Christmas and they fall in love. Yeah, yeah, yeah. Whatever.
"Damn it." The phone rings again.
"Fine, I'll be down in five." I slammed the phone down.
Well, he certainly had the same gene as Christopher. They both knew how to get under my skin. Just in different ways.
Why did I let Jessica talk me into this white bikini? And not bring anything else as a backup. Staring at myself, then putting on my cover-up, I got to cover my flaws.

I get to cabana seven and he's not there. I scan the area to find him talking to two women. They were gorgeous, of course.
 "I'm Robert, your server. Is there anything I can get you?"
For a moment, I thought. "I'll take a Screwdriver and a Pina Colada." I smile. I sit my chair up and people watch. Scanning over to him every so often, watching him interact with the woman who seems to be flirtatious in manner. Rolling my eyes and bringing my attention back to Robert, dropping off my drinks beside me.
"Thank you." I smile. "Robert, can you do me a favor?"
"Sure."
"Do you see that guy over there?"
"You mean Mr. Derby?"
He formally addressed Shane's name.
"Yes. Mr. Derby."
"Can you ask him to repeat these words, Ice Bank Mice Elf?"

Robert looked at me and smiled like he had repeated the words in his head.

"I will make sure you get tipped very well."

He looked like he was thinking about it, then walked off towards Shane.

I watch from afar as Robert whispered to Shane and Shane said something aloud. The women didn't find it amusing as they exited the conversation. Robert and Shane looked my way as I held up my Pina Colada to them with a smile.

"Ice Bank Mice Elf." He sat beside me.

"I figured you did already," I laughed and sipped on my drink.

"Maybe later." He winked.

"TMI."

"Don't you want to get into the pool?" He asked.

"I'm good." Sipping my straw.

"I'm getting in."

He took off his shirt and I stare at him

through my sunglasses and sip my drink continuously.

Robert checked in again and brought me another Pina Colada.

I flipped over, laying on my stomach and closed my eyes.

"What the hell?" I yell, feeling cold water on me.

"You look hot."

"Well, now I'm cold." I flip back over and sit up.

"Why don't you want to get into the pool?"

I flip my sunglasses on top of my head. "Because no one wants to see this mom bod. Seriously, look around. You were even talking to hot chicks."

"They approached me. Plus, I like my women to have meat on their bones. They needed to eat a few cheeseburgers or a pizza. I like something to grab onto, you know."

"Well, okay." I flip my sunglasses back

down and sip on my Screwdriver.
"Well, no one wants to see my stretch marks."
"I'm sure this is all in your head."
"Maybe so, but still."
"You get in the pool with me and I'll have Barney do something messed up to Christopher tonight."
I peeked over my sunglasses, and with the straw in my mouth, contemplating his deal. I mean, if he wasn't here, I would have been in that pool by now because it's hot as hell for December out here.
"Fine. Let's go before I change my mind." Pulling the cover-up over my head, and looked at him.
"Let's go hot guy."
 He didn't move.
"What?"
He just sat there.
 "You're about to give me a complex. Quit staring and come on." Pulling him up off his chair. I wasn't sure why

he stared at me for so long. Maybe my body was as hideous as I felt it was.

He stayed quiet while he followed me into the water.

He seemed to snap out of it once we got in.

"You could have told me it was cold as hell in here."

"You didn't ask?"

"What was up with you back there?" I swam around him, trying to get used to the water.

"Nothing."

"I told you no one wants to see this mom bod."

"You don't have a mom bod," he said.

"Well, your reaction said differently."

"I'm sorry if you thought that was my reaction, but..."

"Look, there's Rosie." Cutting him off and waving to her. "Rosie," I yell too loud. I was so buzzed.

After Rosie left, I continued to swim
and Shane just watched me.
"Robert." I swam to the side of the
pool. "Can I get just one more drink? I
want a Sex on the Beach?"
"Yes, ma'am." He smiled at me.
And I swam to Shane. "For someone
who wanted to get me into this pool,
you sure don't look like you are
having fun. Loosen up." I splash him.
"Come on, have fun." I splash again.
"Fine, I'll just go find another hot guy
to hang with." Turning away. He
grabs me and cradles me.
"You're not going anywhere."
My bare skin touching his burns hot
until he releases me, but I still hold
on. "I had to talk myself down earlier,
if you get my drift," he whispered.
 I released him. "Oh."
"You're turning red." He smiled.
"It's the alcohol."
"Your body is perfect. Don't let
anyone tell you differently."

I see Robert put my drink beside my chair and have the perfect exit from this conversation.

Laying back in my chair, the drinks were having their full effects on me. It finally relaxed me, closing my eyes.

"Wakey, wakey, sleepyhead,"
I hear him say, "Pizza."
I get a whiff of something coming by my nose.
"Yum, pizza," I say with my eyes still closed.
"Figured you needed something to soak up the alcohol."
"Probably so. That was the best nap I've had in ages." I try not to stare at him but I couldn't help it.
"Rosie's going to keep Daisey tonight for you."
"Why?" I ask, getting a piece of pizza.
"Why not? I asked her and she said yes."

"You can't make decisions for my daughter for me," I snap.
"I wasn't I just figured you could use a night with a grown-up."
"I'm around grown-ups all the time at work," I say, stuffing my mouth with the pizza.
"We are going out tonight," he plainly states.
I cut my eyes over to him and put down my pizza.
"One." Holding up a finger. "You don't make decisions about my daughter." Holding up another finger.
"Two. If you want to ask me out, you ask, don't tell."
"I didn't..."
Gathering my things in my arms.
"Three." Holding up three fingers.
"You don't get to use my daughter to woo me." I walk away.
"Dalilah." I hear my name but keep on walking, thinking this trip was a huge mistake.

One Hot Momma

$\mathcal{A}$ knock on the door pulled me from the mushy Christmas movie I was watching. Another woman falls in love with some rich guy who hates Christmas and she changes him. They live happily ever after blah, blah, blah. This time, the knock was louder. "Coming."
Opening the door. "Ms. Foster?" The gray-haired man asked, dressed in a black suit and name tag that read Charles. He had two boxes in his hands.

"Yes."

"These are for you." Holding the boxes out for me to take.

"Thank you, Charles." I smile and take the red and gold boxes.

The label on the boxes were from the boutique we got our dresses from. I slowly untie the golden bow on the bigger red box and popped the top off. Unfolding the tissue paper appeared the dress that I had picked out. Thinking maybe it was a gift from Rachel, I smiled.

I slowly untie the red bow on the smaller gold box. There was a note on top.

I'm sorry. Can I have a redo?

Unfolding the tissue paper were shoes and a necklace and earrings that matched.

I knocked on the conjoining door. Not giving him time when he opened it.

"Four." Holding up four fingers.

"Buying expensive gifts doesn't woo

me, nor is it a genuine apology." I
slam the door.
"Damn it, woman." He barged in.
"What do you want?" He asked.
"What do you want?" He asked again.
"Are you freaking Notebooking me?"
I arched my brow.
"Maybe? Is it working?"
"Five." Holding up all five fingers.
"Don't ever Notebook me again."
"What about Dirty Dancing?"
He asked.
"Unless you can dance like Patrick
Swayze. Then no." I shake my head.

"Listen, I'm sorry. I didn't want to
screw this up, and I have seemed to."
He got down on his knees. "Please go
on a date with me?"
I shake my head at this stupid scene.
"Get up and ask me."
"Dalilah Foster, will you go on a date
with me?"
"I don't know. You see, I need to

wash my hair tonight," I tease.

"I promise not to break any of your five rules tonight."

"See, the thing is, there's a movie I just can't miss coming on."

"What if I tell you there will be ice cream and fireworks on this date?"

"Now see, that's not fair. I guess I will go on a date with you, Shane Derby."

"Can you be ready by four?"

"Sure."

"See you at four." He smiled and walked back to his room.

The now sober me was second-guessing this date looking at myself in the mirror. I hadn't been on a proper date in over a year. I was nervous. Nervous that I was going to crash and burn because of this date. The past two days have pushed us into a place we once had left things, a friendship. The knowledge that we had a chemistry that wasn't ever acted on all those years ago, that's what scared me the most.

With a knock on the door, I check everything again before opening it.

"Wow. You. Look." He stopped and scanned me with a smile. "Beautiful."

"Thank you. You don't look so bad yourself." I take my time looking at him from head to toe.

His black pants and his white dress shirt were untucked. He had a casual but had a dressy tone going on and I liked it. Letting him in, I could tell he was as nervous as I was.

"For you." He handed me a red rose.

"Did you snatch this from the bouquet in the hallway?"

"I plead the fifth." He grinned.

"Thank you." I put the flower in some water.

"You ready."

"Yes."

The nervous energy was palpable in the elevator down to the lobby. It was like we didn't know how to act around each other like this.

"What do you have planned, Mr. Derby?" I ask as we walk along the street lined with Christmas decor.

"No plans."

"You mean to tell me that nothing is planned?"

"Well, the fireworks, but that's thanks to Disney. Only if you want to watch them."

"You had me dress up and we aren't going anywhere?"

"I didn't tell you to wear the dress. That was your decision. Plus, I promised I wouldn't break your five..." He held up his hand. "Rules tonight. So I canceled the reservations I had made and the Cinderella horse and carriage."

"Cinderella Carriage? You were planning to go all out tonight, weren't you?"

"Maybe."

"I don't need those things. I like

simple."

"Well, we will simply walk until we see something that looks fun to do."

"This is killing you, isn't it?" Looking at him. He was a planner and hated to go on a whim.

"Just a little."

"Not everything has to be planned."

"I'm just so used to working like that. It's falling into my lifestyle now."

"Have fun. Don't worry about what time something is and where you need to be."

"Come on." I pull him into the bar. I had my sights on the neon sign for the last block. It's the one place that hasn't looked Disney-related that we've walked by, although I'm sure there's something about it, that is. The music was loud and the dance floor crowded when I pull him onto it.

"I know you have better moves than this," I teased, moving with him.

"The moves I have aren't made for the dance floor."
I could feel the heat run over me.
"Your turning red."
I stayed silent as I moved.

"Spontaneity is key to fun," I say when we walk out of the club.
"I think I'm ready for that ice cream. This hot mamma needs something to cool off." Fanning my face.
"You are one hot momma," he replied. I roll my eyes.
"You don't take compliments well, do you?" He asked.
"Not really. It's just weird."
"Have you thought about the talent scout any?"
"No." I hadn't other than when I thought he had something to do with it.
"What did he say it was for?"
"An animated musical. He liked my voice, he thought it would be a good

fit."

"You should look him up just to make sure it's legit. There are all kinds of scams out there. What was his name?" He pulled out his phone.

"Michael Martin. Martin Talents." I watched him type it into his phone. And he scrolled through the page.

"He looks legit. Just be careful. It looks like he would make a percentage after they pay you, so that sounds like he is legit. Never give anyone money upfront. That person is a scammer," he warned. "I see it all the time in real estate."

"Do you ever see yourself coming back home?"

"No, I love it here in Florida. Other than hurricane season, that's the only downside. We have tropical weather all the time. What's not to love?"

"Do you ever see yourself moving from home?"

"I would love to, but I can't take

Daisey away from Christopher. I would never do that to them. Regardless of how I feel towards him, I couldn't do that."

He nodded his head. "I see your point."

For a moment, I stop. "I could use that horse and carriage right about now." I pull the heels off for some relief.

"There's a bench." He pointed. "How about you sit and I go get the ice cream?"

Slipping the shoes back on and walking to the bench. He whistled when he walked away, swaying his head from side to side. I smiled because that was something he did when he was happy. The sun was setting as I slip my phone out of my purse. I check in with Rachel on Daisey. The photo dump she sent made me sad and happy at the same time. They looked like they were having fun. Part of me wanted to go and the other part was glad I didn't.

"There you go, Cookies and cream double scoop." He handed me the cone.

"You remembered." I smiled.

"I remember a lot of things."

"I wish I could forget some things. But then I wouldn't have Daisey. I believed you made a promise to do something to Christopher. What's the plan?"

"It's a surprise."

"Look at her." I held my phone out to show him the picture of her and Belle. She also had on a Belle dress in the photo.

"She may not realize who made this happen, but thank you. This has been a trip I won't soon forget."

"You know you and her can come down anytime. Maybe for her birthday, you can bring her back here. Or maybe you can come to Port

Charlotte."

"I have no clue what's going to happen in the next six months. I have to find a job and then, with them getting married, we have to figure out how all that's going to work."

"Do you think she is pregnant?"

"Yeah, I do."

"Do you want more kids?" He asked.

"With the right person, yes. I've already learned my lesson. Truthfully, it's been a while since I've been on an actual date. I've met some people from dating apps, but I won't even tell you those horror stories. I'm very picky."

"How about you, been on any dates lately?"

"Sadly, no."

"You're a handsome guy. I'm surprised the ladies don't fall at your feet."

"They do."

"Well, that wasn't cocky at all," I say,

licking my cone.

"I'm just not interested in them."

"What? You're staring at me again." He smiled. "Just watching you lick that cone."

"Oh my god, really." I feel my face flush.

"It's so easy to make you turn red."

"Whatever. You better be glad I didn't just shove it in your face. Any other person I would have."

"So, I'm special."

"Maybe." I smile. "I know you are just playing, most of the time. It's kind of how I got fired from Eddies. A guy slapped my ass. Then wanted me to sit on his lap like he was Santa. Let's just say my stiletto came very close to his family jewels."

"Nice. Sounded like he had it coming to him."

"He did."

"You ready to walk back?" He asked.

I stood up. "I think you might have to

carry me back," I tease.
"Okay," he said and whisked me up
off my feet like I was light as a
feather.
"Put me down," I laugh.
He gently set me back down.

As the sun finally disappeared, all the
Christmas lights appeared.
"It's so pretty out here. All I need is
snow and it would be perfect.
It's hard to believe tomorrow is
Christmas. And that Christopher is
getting married. I always thought I
would get married before him."
"You just haven't found the right
person yet."
"He's going to have to find me at this
point."
"Maybe he has."
His words made me stop and I look
into his hazel eyes, reading them.
"You asked me on the bus, was it me?
It was." He tucked a stray strand of

hair away.
"It was me."
"Why?" I ask.
"Because I've always felt a connection with you, Dalilah."
"You don't think it's some Jerry Springer shit? I had a baby with your brother?"
"No. You both made a stupid decision with alcohol involved. I think we all know that there are no feelings between you two."
"This is so fucked up," I say to him.
"Maybe, maybe not."
Our eyes connected. Everything seemed to fall away at that moment when he leans in. I jump back at my phone vibrating in my purse.
"Sorry. It's my phone." Pulling it out.
"It's Rachel," I say answering the video call.

Buzz Cuts

The moment was gone once I hung up from my call. Well, I should say Daisey's call with Shane.

"You just broke rule three."

"What was rule three?"

"Not using her to woo me."

"If that was wooing you, then this is going to be easier than I thought. We're besties. What's wrong with that?"

"It's just I don't bring men around and I don't want her to get attached."

"Well, I'm her uncle, so I think it's okay. That sounds like some Jerry

Springer shit."
"See." Looking at him. "It's totally messed up. Try to explain it out loud. I had a one-night stand. The one-night stand left me a single mom and now all I can do is think about hopping on his brother's schlong."
 He looked at me.
"I said that last part out loud, didn't I?"
"Yeah." He smiled.
 "Can we forget that part?"
"Not a chance."
"Of course, you wouldn't."

As we took in the lights on the way back, my mind raced with the pros and cons of this becoming more. I knew this would be a long-distance relationship, which was a big con, but I also knew he was good with Daisey, which was a huge pro.

"What time are the fireworks?" I ask stepping in the elevator.

"Around nine."

"You want to watch from the balcony?" I ask.

"My place or yours?"

"I don't know. We have so far to go." I laugh. "Yours, since my room has dolls everywhere."

"Sounds like a plan." His grin beamed with joy.

"You just couldn't help it, could you?"

"Nope." He smiled.

"I'm going to check on Daisey and change."

"Sounds good. See you at nine."

"Momma, momma!" Daisey ran to the door when I walked in. "You look pretty, momma."

I smile. "You do too."

She twirled in her Belle dress. "Rachel got me a Cinderella dress, too."

"Oh, wow." Smiling at her.

"Guess what, Momma?"

"What?"

"I'm going to be a big sister!"

"Really."

 "Yeah. Daddy and Rachel told me today, but it's a secret," she whispered.

Never tell a five-year-old a secret, ever. "Baby, you know you aren't supposed to tell secrets."

"But I tell you everything." She smiled.

"I know. And I always want you to tell me everything." I will save this conversation for another day as I stand up.

"You be good for grandma and I will come to get you when I get up. Okay?"

"Okay," she said, twirling in the dress.

After talking with Rosie about getting
Daisey to bed early for the big day
tomorrow, I walk back to my room
when I had an idea.
I give the front desk the box and
Shane's room number with a smile on
my face.
Tapping on the door, hoping he has it
on. He probably thought it was a
practical joke, which it was, but it
would be something for us to laugh
at.

He opened the door when I truly
belly laughed so hard that I couldn't
talk as I leaned on the doorway.
"You think this is funny?"
"Yep."
"Just remember, payback is a bitch."
The elf costume was too much for me
to handle as I continue to laugh.
"Please go change, so I can take you
seriously," I ask. "I can't with that
on."

He walks away while I continue my
laughing episode.
"Can you leave on the hat?" Asking as
he changes.
"Is this better?" He walked out with
his hat on and those gray sweatpants.
"You are in pajamas, so I figured I'd
be in mine." He smiled.
I knew my face was red because
every part of me was on fire.
"Can you at least put on a shirt?"
I heard a loud boom. "It's starting." I
smile, opening the curtain for the
sliding door.
"I didn't break the rules," he said.

He had the balcony set up like a
picnic, with pillows and a blanket. A
plate of fruit and cheeses with a
bottle of wine.
"We have an hour before Christopher
comes."
"Why is Christopher coming?"
"Rachel wants to stay in different

rooms tonight since it's the night before the wedding."

"Christopher is always messing up my hopes," I say under my breath, taking a strawberry.

"Wine?" He asked.

"No, thank you." Choosing to stay sober so I could take this all in and him.

"I think we should do this every Christmas. Start a Christmas tradition. We used to do cookies when I was little and decorate them with my mom, before she got sick."

"Why don't you do that now?"

"I'll burn down the house. Daisey was two when I did it, and I set off all the fire alarms. Since then, I haven't tried.

"Why don't we do it tomorrow night after the wedding? I'm sure mom would love that. We can put her in charge of the oven."

"That sounds nice."

"Another strawberry?" He asked. Holding one to my mouth and I bite it.

"I've enjoyed tonight," I say, knowing it was getting closer to the end.

"Not that I wouldn't have liked what you had planned, but I'm not the only one that needed to let loose."

"I did too. I had more fun today than I had in a while. I think I need to remember not everything has to be planned out."

"No, it doesn't. I bet you even had it planned down to the perfect kiss." I smile when he didn't deny it.

"Some things you just can't plan."

I lean in. "But sometimes things are worth the wait." My lips touch his, making the first move as the fireworks light up the sky. He fisted my hair and pulled me closer.

His phone lit up, and we both groaned when we saw who the text was from.

I was in the kitchen when he let
Christopher in, making my way back
to my room. "Are you fucking my
brother?" He snapped off before I
made it to my doorway.
"If I was, it wouldn't be any of your
business."
"Bro, what's your problem?" Shane
asked with a slap on the side of his
head.
"I think I should know if you two are."
"It's none of your business if we are,"
I replied. It is just like him to ruin my
good mood.
"It's my business if he's going to be in
Daisey's life."
"Oh, just like it's my business that you
knocked up your fiancée.
Congratulations on the new baby. If
you wanted to keep it a secret, I
wouldn't have told a five-year-old.
Why don't you worry about your life
and I will worry about mine?"
I slammed the door. Then opened it

back, walking through and to the balcony.
"I'll take this." Holding up the bottle and slamming the door again behind me. It wasn't the wine I wanted as I popped it open and filled the glass.

"Fuck it." I opened the door again and walked to Shane, planting a massive kiss. "Goodnight," I say, catching my breath.
"Goodnight dickhead."
I slammed the door for the last time.

I don't know what time I heard a tap on the door that woke me.
Unlocking the conjoining door.
"What?" Saying sleepily when his lips touched mine, walking me backward into the room.

Feeling blissful and cheery for Christmas morning, I heard yelling

from Shane's room.
"What's going on in here?" I open the door, seeing Christopher's head. I cover my mouth to stop my laughter.
"You." He pointed to me.
"You did this, didn't you?"
He pointed to his head.
"That fucking elf shaved my head. We all know you are the one behind the elf shit."
"I wish I could take credit for this. God, I do." Holding in my laughter.
"Where's Shane?" He asked. "If it wasn't you, where the fuck is my brother?"
"How should I know?"
"He's in there, isn't he?" He walked in.
"No." I walked behind him. Looking at the streak going down the middle of his head that was buzzed cut. Inwardly I was dying inside of laughter, knowing if I started I wouldn't stop.

"Stay still." I turn his head back.
"Unless you want a gapped-up
hairdo, don't move again." I buzz the
back of Christopher's head.

He all but cried that we were going to
ruin the wedding for Rachel. I,
unfortunately, felt bad for Rachel, so I
told him I would fix his hair. Now if I
knew where my elf partner in crime
was, leaving me here to fix his mess.
I needed to have a small heart-to-
heart with Christopher while we were
alone.

"Can I talk to you about something?"
"It's about Shane, isn't it?"
I see him look at me in the mirror.
"Yeah," I sigh.
"I'm not an idiot, Dalilah. I knew you
had a thing for him back then." He
paused. "When he asked to invite you
on this trip, I wasn't oblivious to

where this could go. It was pretty obvious on the way here you two have a connection."

"So you are okay if we pursue a relationship?" Stopping and looking at his reflection in the mirror. He turned to me. "I just want you to be happy. I want Daisey to have someone that's there for her. I want someone that will take care of her and I know he would."

"All done." I buzz the last part.

"Sorry if I was a dick last night."

"I'm used to it. I've got to go get Daisey. If you need me to help with anything for the wedding, let me know."

"Dalilah," he said before I step back into my room.

"Yeah." Turning to look at him.

"I think I've seen you the happiest I've seen you in a while and if it's Shane, then you should be with him."

"Thanks." Closing the door with a smile.

Dreaming of a White Christmas

The loud hotel phone rings.
"Ms. Foster?"
"Yes."
"Mr. Derby is requesting you to meet him in the lobby immediately."
"Okay. Thank you."

Looking like a hot mess, I pulled my hair up and went down to the lobby.
"Where have you been?" I hit him on the arm. "Leaving me to clean up your mess with Christopher."
"What are you doing?" He put a blindfold on me. I pulled it down.
"You know I had to freaking buzz cut his hair. Where were you?"
"Just put it back on."

"Fine," I huff.

He maneuvers me. "Where are we going?" Feeling the wind hit me.

"Just a few more steps. Tell me what you feel?"

"Pissed I just had to spend my morning with Christopher."

"Besides that. Hold out your hand."

"I'm starting to think you are crazy. What I'm I supposed to feel?" Something cold hits my hand and arms. He pulls off my blindfold.

"Merry Christmas," he whispered to me.

I smile and held out my hands, feeling the snow hit them and laugh. "How?" I twirled as the machine blew the snow out and it floated gently to the ground. Only to melt moments later. It was beautiful.

"I think Daisey would love this." I smile. "She's already on her way down."

"Thank you." Standing on the tips of

my toes and kissing him under the snow.

"I believe Santa has some gifts back in Grandma's room," Shane announced.
"Presents!" Daisey jumped up and down, catching the snow with two other kids that have made their way to our little winter heaven.

While Daisey, Shane, Christopher, Rachel, and Rosie played, I cleaned the mess of all the wrapping paper. It made me happy that we all got to enjoy her this morning together. It wasn't normal to be all together as a family. "Daddy, why did you cut your hair?"
"Well, before Barney left, he told me I should cut it for the wedding."
"I'm going to miss him," she said.
I shake my head. I would not miss him. "I'm not," I say lowly, stuffing

the paper into the trash can.

The Wedding

"Momma?" Daisey asked as I was fixing her hair for the wedding.
"What?"
"Is daddy going to have time with me now that he's getting married and having a baby?"
I stopped and leaned down. "Of course, he will. His heart is just growing bigger. He will always have time and space for you." Her question made my heart ache.
"He loves you so much, we all do," I assured her.
"What about you and daddy?"
Her question confused me.
"What about us?"
"Why didn't you get married?"
Oh boy, a five-year-old couldn't understand our situation and I don't

know if I would ever tell her the story.

"Sometimes people love each other in different ways. Your dad and I love each other. Ours is a friendship type of love." Making it sound nicer than it was. Sure, I cared for him, but love is not what I ever felt for him.

"Are you going to get married?"

"No, honey. First, you have to fall in love with someone."

"Do you love Shane?"

The thing about kids is they ask, say, and do anything.

"No, baby. We are just friends," I answered her question honestly, but friends don't kiss like we did last night. Could I see myself falling for him and his ways? Of course.

"Momma. Shane's here." She twirled
herself around in her burgundy dress,
into the bathroom, and out.
 "Okay." Putting the finishing touches
on my makeup.
Twirling back in she stopped.
"Can I wear lipstick today?"
"Come here." Taking my lip gloss out.
"That's not lipstick, this is?" She
handed me the tube.
"You have to stop watching YouTube
so much." Putting it on her.
"Good?" I ask.
"Yep." Moving her lips together and
popping her p.
"Okay, we are ready."
 We walk out of the bathroom, seeing
him in his black tuxedo. My eyes
perused him with dirty thoughts,
which I had to quickly erase as the
heat flowed through me.
"Doesn't he look handsome?"
Daisey said.
"Yes, he does."

"Shane, doesn't momma look pretty today?"

"What? I don't look pretty every day?" I tease.

"No." She looked at me.

"Gee, thanks." I shake my head at her genuine statement.

"Yes, your mom looks pretty, even in her pajamas. "

"You haven't seen the pajamas she wears at home."

"Daisey," I scold her.

"What, Momma? He hasn't. They have holes and are ripped." She shrugged her shoulders. "It has some dude named Nirvana it."

"You mean Kurt Cobain?" Shane asked.

"I don't know." She expressed with her hands.

He looked at me and he knew what shirt it was. It was the one I got on our all-state drama trip. I spilled a drink on my shirt and he had worn it under his dress shirt. He smiled knowingly at me.

"What? I have a thing for Kurt. I refused to let him go."

Never did I think when I got on that bus I would be walking down an aisle with Shane beside me, in a wedding. Never would I think I would be smiling at this moment once I agreed to do this as Shane tells me stupid dirty jokes walking towards the front. Daisey was just a few paces ahead, throwing white rose petals high into the air with each twirl. It was her spin of being the flower girl.

Turning to the seats seeing Rosie sitting up front with Rachel's parents. I never cry at weddings but tears found their way out. Standing beside Rachel, whose vows to Christopher were beautifully said. Almost sickeningly beautiful. She sees so much more in him than I ever did. The words she spoke were a love story on its own. Meeting Shane's eyes, thinking about the last few days. I knew what I wanted was standing just paces away, and I was the only thing stopping it.

Mistletoe Kisses & Christmas Cookies

The simple decorations of red poinsettias and white roses on the tables. The simple white cake seemed to glitter against the glow of the small amber fairy lights.

As we watched them, the newly married couple was swaying to the music. Daisey was busy twirling in her dress around them on the dance floor.
"Can we have cake yet?" Daisey spun to me.
"Sure, whenever they finish dancing."
Or sucking face.
"Go ask your dad." Was that rude of

me to suggest? Maybe, as she twirled over to them.

"Momma, come dance with me." Daisey tugged on me.
"Okay, okay." After her third attempt, I caved in.
"No, momma like this," Daisey instructed me on how to twirl properly.
"Momma is going to get sick if she keeps twirling," I say, spinning one last time for her.
"Can you teach me some twirling skills?" Shane asked, saving me as I mouth thank you to him.

"He's really good with her," Rosie said to me as I watch them.
"Yeah," I sigh, leaning on my hand, watching them.
"You know, when I was young, I dated a boy."

I wasn't in the mood for a story about who she dated, but I continued to listen.

"I wouldn't call what I had with that boy love, but he had a handsome brother."

Now she has caught my attention.

"I knew it was wrong to pursue his brother after we had broken up. Then, ten years later, on one hot summer day down at the lake, he was there, and came over to talk to me. His brother had long moved on and gotten married to some floozy, but that's another story. Anyway, he asked me out, and I said yes. Six months later we were married." She smiled looking over to me. "Sometimes you can't help who you fall for. I'm going to go dance with my son." She got up and walked to the dance floor, stealing Christopher away from Rachel, leaving me to think about things.

"May I have this dance?" Shane
asked, holding out his hand. I smile
and take it.
Swaying to the slow song, I leaned my
head on his chest, listening to his
heart and the music.
"This would never work," I say.
"Why not?"
"You're here and I'm there."
"Is that the only reason?" He asked.
Other than my own insecurities, yes.
"You don't think it's breaking a
brother code or something?"
"He's the one that broke it first."
He had a point.

"Cake time." Daisey clapped with joy.
"I guess it's cake time," I say, not
wanting to pull away.
"But first." He smiled and looked up.
He didn't give me a chance to stop
the public sediment.

"Momma, you were kissing Shane,"
she said with a mouthful of cake.
"Uh-huh," I answered with my mouth
full of cake. Whatever was going on
was now public knowledge. Although
I was the only one that was seemingly
still on the fence about what to do
about my feelings for Shane.

"It's supposed to look like this."
Daisey pointed at the cookie that
they had decorated. They perfectly
colored the candy cane in with its red
and white stripes.
The gift I'm wearing distracted me.
The elf suit was just horrendous, but I
wore it since he was wearing his,
guessing this was his payback. It
wasn't so bad knowing it had put a
smile on Daisey's face.
"Here's the last pan." Rosie pulled out
the batch of cookies for us.

"This was a good idea," Rachel said. I did not know this would be a family thing when I agreed to this. I had assumed that they would have a traditional wedding night.

"So you and Shane?" She whispered to me. Shrugging my shoulders to her, I wasn't sure what we were yet.

"You should totally go for it." She smiled and went back to where Christopher was.

"You should totally go for it," Shane whispered.

"You should totally not be eavesdropping," I replied.

"My little elf needs some attention."

"If that's an innuendo."

"You're a naughty elf." He smiled.

"Momma, what do you think?" Daisey came up to us. "Oh, my," laughing, her little elf costume was too cute.

"Awe, look at you all. I have to get a picture," Rachel said excitedly. "Say

cheese whiz."
I laugh as we all say it, standing close together.
 "One more with just you two." I stood beside him to pose. "A little closer to each other," she instructed. "This isn't working for me. Where's the Christmas Cheer at?" She said.
I was about to Christmas Cheer her if she just didn't take the picture. "Stand here." She moved me in, facing him, into the archway in the kitchen. "Now say mistletoe." Shane took the queue with his lips touching mine.

Who Knew Elves Could be So Sexy

After the sugar rush of the cake and cookies wore off, Daisey passed out in the bed. I, on the other hand, sat on the balcony enjoying the warm air and the sights of the lights that I could see twinkling in the night.
I look down at the pictures that Rachel sent me contemplating what I should or shouldn't do.
The smile on my face said so much in those pictures, so why was I second-guessing it? If it was just me, I would just go with it, but I had to think about the consequences if this didn't work out. How awkward everything would be with Christopher's family was my major concern.

"Come in," he said with my tap on his door.

"I can't believe you still have that on." Looking at him with the elf outfit still on.

"Here, wear this." He put the elf hat on me.

"What are you doing?"

"Taking it off." He smiled, taking the shirt off.

 I stared as if I'd never seen his bare chest before, bringing my thoughts to why I was here, leaning on the kitchen bar. "Can we talk?"

"Sure," he said, taking off the pants next.

"Fucking elf boxers," I say when he grabbed the hat back and put it on his head and wiggles his brows.

"These are boxer briefs," correcting me.

"Whatever." Shaking my head, getting back to my point. "I don't want Daisey to be affected if this

doesn't work out. You two have a bond. I don't want that to go away."
"It won't, I promise." He looked me in the eye.
"How can you make that promise? You don't know what's going to happen. It's not just me that I'm scared that will get heartbroken."
"Listen, I would never do anything to hurt Daisey or you."
"Intentionally, sure, you can say that."
"I like you a lot, Delilah. The last few days have been great with you and Daisey."
"I have too, more than I'd like to admit." Inhaling deeply, trying to keep my eyes from roaming him.
"When I came on this trip, none of this was expected. Them. You. Us." Looking over at him.
"What are you thinking?"
"How hot elves can look," I say with a smile.

"It's the hat, isn't it?"
I shook my head no. I didn't intend to act on anything I was feeling. Trying to keep myself in check was getting harder and harder.
"The present the elf is holding." My direct observation made him turn red. "Although I find the gray sweats more of a turn-on."
"Noted." He stood in front of me. "Tell me more."
"More what?" His body is close enough I feel the heat radiating from him.
"What turns you on?"
There were so many ways I could answer this, but it was all that he had shown me the past few days. His laugh, his need to make me smile, the way he was with Daisey, and the way he listened to what I said.
"Your heart," I said, putting my hand on his chest. "Your mind, dirty and all." I laugh. "Tell me what turns you

on?" Biting my lip, maybe pushing this conversation somewhere there would be no turning back from. "Your sense of humor, your mind. Your need to be independent." Our eyes locked. I was being drawn into him. "Your lips." He brushed his to mine.

"Momma." Daisey sleepily walked into his room, rubbing her eyes. Shane quickly took his hat off and covered himself.
"Yeah baby, let's go back to the room." I scooted her back to the door, turned, and mouthed sorry to him. Kids are also the biggest cock blocker ever.

Christmas Isn't Over Yet

I searched on my phone while lying beside Daisey, waiting for her to go to sleep again. Scrolling through the Martin Talents site seeing the email for contact info, and hit the icon. I hovered over the screen, second-guessing to do this or not.
Quickly typing in the required info and a small statement to Mr. Martin himself, before I changed my mind. I was sure my information wouldn't make it pass his assistant and if it did, he wouldn't remember me. I hit send and smile at my accomplishment for tonight.

Looking over at my baby girl, her curls splayed across the pillow, I move slowly and gently not to wake her.

Tapping lightly on his door before opening it. "You awake?"
I whispered, stepping into the kitchen.
"Yeah, why are you whispering?"
He whispered back, sitting up in his bed.
"It would be rude to yell."
"It's rude to just walk uninvited into someone's room." He pointed out.
"I can just go back." Turning around.
"I was just teasing. My door is always open for you. "
He needed to stop saying all the right things.
"Hop in." He moved the covers for me to join him. "I promise I won't bite." He smiled.
"I might want to be bit," I tease back, sitting safely on the end of the bed,

tucking one leg under me and facing him to talk.

"I emailed Mr. Martin." Playing with the edge on the pillow.

"I'm glad. You deserve to reach for your dream."

"I doubt if he will even know who I am. I'll just be in a stack of emails, but I put it out there."

"I'm sure he will remember you. You're hard to forget."

I roll my eyes. "Why do you always know exactly what to say?" Paying more attention to the pillow than him.

"It's not hard when you mean them." He's giving me that smile that makes me melt when I look up.

"I'm really going to miss our little talks," I say, knowing tomorrow we head home and our time is running out.

"Who said we can't still have our talks?"

I stay silent because my mind has been all over the place with what could go wrong and how.

"I know you are thinking about what could go wrong, but why not just see what happens?"

"I wish it was that easy for me, but there are consequences if this doesn't work out. I have to think about those."

"Screw the consequences." He pulled my leg, bringing me closer.

"What are you doing?" I laugh.

"Christmas isn't over yet. Getting another Christmas kiss in." His lips met mine and I'm so done.

"Or two," he said after he pulled away and smiled. Before I had time to respond, kissing me again.

I stopped thinking about it all, wrapping myself around him in every way I could.

"You are so beautiful."

"You are just saying that so you can

get laid," saying hovering over him. My lady bits straddling too close to his manhood with my body screaming do it and my mind screaming don't. His hands were on my waist, holding me.

"Would you go on another date with me on Thursday?" He asked.

"Ooh, Thursday is Supernatural night."

"It's a rerun this week."

"But it's one I missed," I tease, knowing it wasn't. I faithfully watch my favorite show. It was the one guilty pleasure I gave myself.

"Well, pizza and Supernatural at my hotel."

"What about Chinese and Supernatural on my couch? I can get a sitter for Daisey."

"How about sushi and Supernatural in your bed?" He slapped my butt.

"Ouch. Are we negotiating our date?"

"Maybe."

"Sushi and Supernatural on my couch and it's a deal."
"You drive a hard bargain." He smiled.
Waking up wrapped in him, I slip his arms from around me and sneak back towards my room. I stop and look at him before closing the door and smile. I smile because even though all we did was talk, kiss, and cuddle, it all felt right.

Wind Blowing in My Hair

Smiling with the wind blowing my hair. "This is so much better than the bus." The convertible felt like freedom on the open road, taking in the smell of the fresh air. "This isn't the way we came." Observing the surroundings, opening my eyes.
"We are dropping mom off at my aunt's. She's staying there for a few weeks."
"Cool." I continued to take in the vitamin D I so badly needed, with my head resting on the seat and a smile.
"You seem awful chipper today."
"It's the sun." I plaster a big smile on

my face when I look at him before closing my eyes again. It wasn't just the sun that had me smiling today.

"Momma, momma wake up. Look, it's the beach." She tapped my seat with excitement. "Can we go, momma? Please, please," she begged, bopping up and down in her seat. "I always wanted to build a sandcastle."

"We've got to get on the road, baby, maybe another day."

"What's a day at the beach going to hurt? I don't have to be at work this week and I'm guessing neither do you?"

He had a point, I no longer had a job to return to, and I wanted to put my feet in the sand. Daisey had never been to a beach before and this would be perfect timing, but I teased before giving my answer. "I have a date Thursday, with a very handsome guy that I just can't miss."

"This guy must be pretty special to want to miss a day at the beach with this hot guy and a Pina Colada," he teased back and winked.

"Momma, what's a date?"

I heard Rosie chuckle from the back seat.

"You know how we go for a playdate to Bella's?" I ask her.

"Yeah."

"Well, dating is like that, but just for grown-ups. When you like someone, you go on a date?"

"So, you go on dates with Jessica?"

"No, baby. Jessica is my friend. My date is with a boy."

"Boys are gross and mean. Why would you want to go with a boy?"

Hearing Rosie chuckle once again, I couldn't help but to laugh with her.

"One day you might change your mind about boys. Let's just hope it's not until you graduate college."

My feet stepped onto the warm sand and the salt air whipped my hair around. "Come on, let's get in the water." Daisey pulled on my arm. "Okay, okay. Let's just go to the edge of the water we have to be careful. The ocean is different from your kiddie pool."

I knew she didn't care what I just instructed her as her little fast legs took off like lightning.

The water splashing against us with each step we take further in holding her on my hip. Her laughter was priceless with each wave that hit us. "Deeper, let's go." Her little legs spurring me to go further into the water.

"You are getting too heavy to hold you like this anymore. Did Santa give you a growth spurt?"

"Don't be a goober momma, he gave
me toys," she giggled and hugged my
neck.
"Look, Shane is coming." She pointed
toward the shoreline, turning to look
and smile.
He had a bucket in tow and a cup as
we met at the shoreline.
"Pina Colada for you and a bucket for
us to build a sandcastle for you."
Handing us our things.
"Go sit and enjoy the drink and we
will build the castle."
"Thank you," I whisper into his ear
with a kiss on his cheek.
He is slowly making his way further
into my heart, and I was dreading
when this trip was going to be over.
Sitting on the towel and watching
them play in the sand, I think of how
things can be if I just let them and
stop overthinking it. I knew he
wouldn't intentionally hurt either of
us, but my track record wasn't the

best with men. With this, I would have to not only protect myself but my daughter from the possible heartache.

I move to join in on building the castle, wanting to take in the moment with both of them.

"We are going to stay here for the night," he announced, making the moat around the castle.

"If it's okay, Daisey can stay with Aunt Marie and mom, and we can go to my place."

"We? Me and you?" Asking nervously.

"You and me, yes."

I can feel my face flush, alone time with him could be dangerous. I think the only reason we didn't cross the line last night was that Daisey was in the next room.

"Would you like to accompany me to my place?" He asked. His eyes told me a lot when I looked at him. I was sure he felt something for me or else he wouldn't be putting in so much effort.

"Yes. I will accompany you, but no monkey business."

"I can't make a promise I might break."

"Me either," I whisper, teasing him.

The last few hours on the beach were full of secret looks, and one stolen kiss that had butterflies fluttering around.

His bare toes tickle my foot under the dinner table, letting out a giggle, and everyone looks at me.

"Thank you for the lovely meal, Mrs. Marie," I say.

"It was my pleasure." Marie smiled and continued to talk about how nice

it was to have family here for the
holidays.
I was happy that Daisey was getting
to meet some of her extended family
on this trip. The house is full of
cousins I never knew existed. It was
almost overwhelming for me to
handle as they introduced me to
everyone.

After dinner, I got Daisey ready for
bed and explained to her I was going
on a trip and would be back in the
morning. Tucking her in the bed, I
lean in to kiss her forehead.
"Goodnight, baby. Love you."
"Love you too, momma. You are the
best momma ever."
"And you are the best, too."

I check my phone before walking to
the car. Hovering over the email
nervously before opening it.

Decisions

"What are you thinking about over there?" Shane asked.

"How far to your place?" I was taking in the fresh salt air of the ocean, knowing that wasn't what I was thinking about, I wanted to let it soak in before I tell him.

I had read the email three times, not believing what I was reading. Mr. Martin wanted to meet with me on Friday. I hadn't planned on him answering my email, much less wanting a meeting for a screen test. This was big, not big, but huge news, and I wasn't sure what to do with it. I knew he would be happy and supportive, but part of me wasn't

sure if I would even go through with
the meeting. In theory, I should, but
the reality is that I don't live here for
this job to work. I would also need a
place to stay until Friday and I had
zero extra funds to spare on a hotel.
"About twenty minutes."
I smile, holding my news and trying to
figure out what to do without his
influence.

We pull into a driveway to a
beautiful, small white beachfront
bungalow. "This is beautiful," I say,
getting out of the car.
"You might not think that when you
go in." He raised his brow.
"Forgive the mess. I wasn't planning
on company," he said, unlocking the
door and letting us in. "Welcome to
my humble abode."
"If you think this is messy, you need
to come to my apartment," I chuckle.
His house was impeccably clean for a

bachelor. "Just wait until you have kids. Your house will never be clean again."

I spoke the truth. My house looked like a tornado had come through it most days, even if I cleaned it that same day. It was a vicious cycle of having a kid, you clean and they mess up.

"Nice place." Looking around the house full of neutral beachy tones.

"Thanks, I've been working on it to flip. I still have a lot of work to do."

"Is that what you do, flip?"

"This is my second. I sold my first and found this one, but this one I've seemed to have fallen in love with. So I'm on the fence about flipping it."

"I can see why, it's a beautiful house and on the beach."

"I have to run to my neighbors right quick. I'll be right back. Make yourself at home. There's beer or wine in the fridge."

I roam the house freely, looking over everything.

"Meet Mr. Whiskers." He holds the cat carrier to my face before opening and the cat meows.
"Why does he have an elf?" I point out in the carrier.
"It's his toy. He doesn't go anywhere without it."
I took the cat in my arms after he pulled him out.
"He's so purrty." I giggle at my play on words and pet the fluffy white cat with green eyes.
Mr. Whiskers jumps off my lap, grabs the elf, and takes it to the cat bed.
"So, now you got me to your house, what are you going to do with me?" Biting my lip and holding my breath. I knew tonight would either begin or end what this was.

His body heat radiated from him.

"First, I'm going to kiss you." His lips brush my neck. "Then I'm going to worship you," his whisper sent goosebumps down my body.

Nothing has ever felt so good as him saying those words. Deciding before we get sidetracked by his plan, I would tell him.

"Earlier you asked what I was thinking about."

"Yeah."

"I got an email from Mr. Martin." Pausing for dramatics.

"And what did it say?" His face lit up with anticipation.

"He wants me to meet with him Friday to do a screen test."

He picked me up with a hug. "See, I knew he would remember you. Just have faith in yourself. You can do this."

"The thing is, I can't afford a hotel until Friday."

"You two can stay here," he offered quickly, without hesitation.
"We couldn't impose on your life like that."
"You all aren't imposing on my life. Have you sent him an answer yet?"
"No."
"Then do it now and we can celebrate."
"I'll do it later." I still hadn't decided if this is a fit for me.
"If you wait, you will just talk yourself out of it."
He is right, I would do exactly that. I would always wonder what if I didn't do it?
"Okay." Pulling up my emails and typing out my response. Hovering over the send button second-guessing the decision, the decision that could be life-changing for us.
"Just do it," he whispered and nibbled on my ear. Closing my eyes, hitting send, and letting butterflies

flutter in my belly for what's coming next.

Elves, Supernatural and the Audition

My eyes popped open and I let out a scream from the meow. It wasn't the cat's meow that scared me. "What the fuck?"

Mr. Whiskers had placed the freaky elf on my chest.

"What's going on?" Shane asked with a yawn.

"Freaking elf."

"Just throw it. He'll be happy."

I toss the elf towards the door and Mr. Whiskers takes off.

I could hear the jingle of the bell from the elf's hat, so I look at the cat. "He's humping the elf."

"What can I say? We're a bunch of horny bachelors." He pulled me back to him, wrapping his arms around me.

"Crispy bacon is served." He sat a tray of food on the bed in front of me.
"You didn't have to cook," saying with a grin, taking the perfectly cooked bacon.
"Marie and mom are bringing Daisey. So we have an hour to spare. What would you like to do?"
I didn't answer, cocking my head with a smile.

"Can we go swimming?" Daisey asked before we even settled in for the next few days. "I've got a call to take, but after that, sure."
"Can I play with the cat?"
"Go for it," Shane said.
The look he gave me made me melt and my stomach fluttered with

butterflies from him and the call I'm waiting on.

"I'm not sure if I'm going to be able to convince her we have to leave Saturday," I say, flopping down on the sofa after reading my lines to Daisey as her bedtime story.
The past few days we have enjoyed the beach, and I have been memorizing lines and a song for my audition. The extended vacation with just us has been full of laughs and memories I will not soon forget.
Popping a California roll into my mouth and flipped the TV to the CW.
"Yum." Humming with delight.
I curled into myself on the sofa and glued my eyes to the TV.
 "You really are into this show," he observed.
"Yes, I never miss it. I even make sure I'm off on Thursday nights."
"What are you going to do now, it's

the last season?"

"Rewatch it a billion times." I smile. "When I can't sleep, I'll put it on Netflix."

"I know something that will tire you out." He arched his brow and smiled.

"I'm sure you do." Popping another roll into my mouth.

I hear the bell of the elf hat jingling after I toss it away from me, after he dropped it on my lap. "At least one of you has a girlfriend now."

 I turn to look at him with his big smile. "What are you grinning so big for?"

His eyes gleamed into mine.

"What?" I ask again.

"You just said you're my girlfriend."

"No, I didn't." I thought about what I had just said.

"I'm not your girlfriend? You haven't asked me." I take my attention quickly back to my show. However, I thought about what I said. I did say I

was his girlfriend. I didn't mean to let
it slip out; those words terrified me.
Playing house the last few days has
been nice, but the real world had
odds stacked against us.

Between going over the song and
lines in my head all night, I couldn't
sleep. I thought that was what had
me up looking through his cabinets
for sweets. I needed something
sweet, something fierce, as I quietly
try to search.
"What are you doing?"
"Shit." Holding my hand to my heart.
"I need something sweet."
"I don't keep a lot of sweets around,
but for emergencies." He opened the
very top cabinet. "They're up here."
Pulling out chocolate chip cookies.
"Milk?" He asked.
"Please." The bag crunched as I tear
into it.

"You nervous about tomorrow?"
"Yeah." Stuffing my mouth with a cookie. I was, but it was my earlier admission is what was bothering me more. It was also bothering that after I said it I told him he had to ask and he hadn't. Maybe he has seen what this would be like the past few days and changed his mind. It was an instant family situation, which is why I brought no one home. Maybe he thought he liked it, but once he got a full dose of what it's like, he had changed his mind.
"Thanks for the cookies." I dip the next in the milk.
"What's bothering you?" He asked, looking hot, shirtless in his gray sweats.
"Nothing." I shove the cookie in my mouth.
"Okay, I'm going back to bed."
He walked off.

I swear, men have no clue whatsoever.

"Try it one more time," the man standing in front of me asked. My nerves and mind were unsettled all morning and I am sure I'm bombing this audition.
I belt out the song one more time to be only cut off midway through.
"Okay, thank you," he dismissed me.
"How'd it go?" Shane asked when I got in the car.
"I'm pretty sure I bombed. They will call back the secretary told me." Leaning my head back on the seat.
"Can we get ice cream now?" Daisey asked from the back. "I've been good the whole time." She smiled that I'm getting what I want smile.
"Sure, baby. Momma needs something sweet, too," I sigh.

"When we get back, we have to pack and clean your mess so we can leave in the morning."

"I don't want to leave. Can't we stay with Shane?"

"No, baby. You have school, and your dad at home."

This is why I didn't want her to get attached to him. This is why I didn't want to open myself up to him, only to be disappointed in the end. Maybe he was more like Christopher than I had thought.

Convenience Store Parking Lot

They filled the ride home with games
of eye spy, and different versions of
the alphabet game, since I forgot to
charge her tablet. I was quiet the first
few hours, then participated in their
games, my mind still preoccupied
with the audition and him.
"Momma, it's your turn."
"Eye spy with my little eye,
something blue."
Daisey started saying all the blue
things she saw and I tell her no.
"The sky," Shane said.

"Yep."

"Let's do story-time now," he said.

"What's story-time?" I ask.

"We all tell a story you have to start with once upon a time. I'll start. Paying little attention to his story, and looked at my phone again, hoping for an email or call to come through. Knowing it was the weekend, it was unlikely I would get an answer.

It got quiet in the car and I turned around to find Daisey fast asleep.

"Now that she's asleep, you want to talk about what's bothering you?"

"Nope." Turning back to my phone, flipping through the pictures from the trip. My heart sinks with each one I look at.

"Once upon a time there was this boy who liked a girl. The boy always knew the girl was meant for him, but life took them away from each other. Then one magical day he was able to

see her again, only this time he knew he would not leave quietly. He was going to make his mark on her heart like she had done on his unknowingly."
He glanced at me, making sure he had my attention.
"This girl wasn't the girl that he left any longer. She was a woman that now had a child. Now she loved her little girl so much that she always put her little girl before herself and happiness. He knew if he tried hard enough, he could make her smile and find her happiness again. What he didn't expect was to fall for her and her daughter so hard. Now he had to once again leave, but not willingly. And not without trying to convince her that this could work. There was one question he wanted to ask her, but out of fear she would say no, he hadn't."
I was listening and holding on to

every word, that I didn't even realize that he had pulled off the main highway and put the car in park.

 "I'll be right back." He leaped out of the car.

What the hell? He just gave me this story and now he's running into a convenience store. Did it scare him that much that I would say no?

Should I just ask him? He got me to break down my walls, smile, and laugh again. He gave me hope that all men weren't assholes.

I got out when he opened my door and gestured for me to do so. Softly closing the door so we could talk.

"What's wrong?"

"Nothing."

"Then why are we standing here?"

Crossing my arms, I'm confused by his behavior the last twenty-four hours he's been hot and cold. Then he just gave me a story that had me believing he wanted to move forward.

He wipes the sweat from his forehead. "It's hot, you hot?"

"I'm fine. What's wrong with you?" I smirk and shake my head. It was warm but not hot.

"Okay, I got this." Giving himself a pep talk.

"You got what? Seriously, are you feeling well?" Mom mode kicked in when I reached to feel his forehead. "Jesus, how do people do this on the fly?"

"I think you've been driving too long, here get in and I'll drive."

I turn to open the door so he will get in, the car beeps when he locks the door.

"Why did you do that?" Asking when I turn back towards him. "What are you doing?" Asking with him on one knee.

"Dalilah, I can't take you back home without you knowing I want this. I want you. I want Daisey. I want us. I want you to know you are it and I want you to be my wife."

He pulled out a ring pop. "Will you marry me?"

"You can't do this here?"

"I think I just did. So will you marry me? It can be a long engagement or short, whatever you want."

My heart pounded at this insanity that was taking place in a convenience store parking lot as I nod yes. "Yes."

The kiss in the parking lot had an old lady telling us to get a room.

"You know I need a ring that's not edible."

"That was all I had to choose from in there," he laughed.

My heart pounded thinking that I just got engaged on a whim. I told him the best things aren't planned.

Never did I think he would ask me to marry him. Were we crazy? Maybe, but I was crazy for him and had always been.

Christmas in July

It was ten days after we got home that I got the call from Mr. Martin that I landed the part in the animated film. I would like to think it was also that day that turned my life in a new direction, but it wasn't. It was ten days prior in a convenience store parking lot.

"You ready?" He called to me.

"Give me a minute, you're rushing me. You can't rush perfection," I laugh.

We take turns traveling to each other, more him than me. This is my third trip down to work on the film and this time it was just us. Rachel wanted Daisey to stay with them for the summer. The separation anxiety has had me on pins and needles, leaving her for so long. Why Rachel thought it would be a good idea to have a six-year-old and newborn at the same time was beyond any logic I could comprehend.

"Ready." I step out of the bathroom.

"Wow!" He kisses me. "Beautiful." He kisses me again. "Perfection."

I pull away. "If you keep on, we won't make it out the door tonight."

"I can live with that." He kisses me again.

"I didn't get dressed up like this just to stay in. Where are you taking me tonight?" Drinking in the sight of him in the suit he was wearing.

"It's a surprise."

"But first I have a gift for you, for later." Handing me a box wrapped in Christmas paper.

"You didn't have any other paper to wrap it in?"

"Just open it."
I tear into the paper and open the
box. "You are crazy if you think I'm
putting this on later." Holding up the
sexy elf outfit. "It's not even
Christmas yet."
"It's called Christmas in July."
"Even if it was Christmas in
December, I won't be wearing this."
Closing the box and putting it down.
I hear the jingle of the elf hat. "Do
you both have elf fetishes?"
He shrugged his shoulders and grabs
my hand. "We're going to be late," he
said, pulling me along.
"You sure are in a hurry tonight."
"Seven sharp."
 Is all he said.
"It's only six. We have an hour."

"Here, put this on." He handed me
my sleep mask that said *Fuck off* on
it. "Why?"

"It's a surprise."
"Fine." Slipping it over my eyes.
The car stops and I hear him get out and open my door.
"Where are we?"
"Just go with it and stop asking so many questions," he whispered into my ear, sending goosebumps down my body. I've may have found something to try later with the sleep mask.
"I hear Christmas music."
"What do you feel?" Whispering again in my ear.
I was about to say something naughty, but I thought better of it, not knowing where we were.
"Cold air."
"What else?"
"Is it raining?"
"No." I feel him take my hand.
"What do you feel now?"
"Crazy," I laugh. I could feel something going around my finger.

I slip the mask off and my eyes take a moment to adjust.

Looking at him kneeling on his knee, I feel tears forming, looking at the ring and back at him.

"Will you marry me?"

"Yes." I had no doubt this time that I would marry him. I did not doubt that he loved us as I take in the moment looking at him and the surroundings. They decorated the area with an elf Christmas theme and a snow machine. It was us. We fell in love at Christmas and it is perfect. He is elfing perfect, as we kiss.

My white princess dress looked like it was from one of those cheesy Hallmark Christmas movies that I so despise. My life had turned into one the last two years. A whirlwind romance engagement, to following my dream of singing. It was all I had ever dreamed of and more.

"Ready," Jessica asked.

"Yes." Looking at myself in the mirror.

"Momma, you look like a princess," Daisey said.

"So do you, baby." I kiss her cheek when I lean to her.

"You remember what to do?" I ask

her.
"Yep." She twirled in her white dress that was like mine.

The music started, and Daisey twirled down the aisle and threw the white rose petals in the air. My heart melts when he takes her hand at the end and they both look at me.
The twinkle in his eyes calms my nerves taking Daisey's hand to join us as a family, as the officiant starts the ceremony bonding us forever.
Everything is perfect, just like a dream that I was still waiting to wake up from.
It wasn't until we got to the reception that I saw the complete madness that had taken place.
Word to the wise, never let the groom have complete control over anything in your wedding.
Elves, elves, and more elves. They are everywhere, doing all the things I had

done the past few years.

I look at my now husband. "You had one thing to get right."

"It's Barney's fault."

"Yeah, blame the elf." Shaking my head. "And where is Barney?" Looking at all the elves and the mess they had made. I hear Rachel laughing and Jessica in the background.

"Well, he asked Barbie to marry him. He wanted to do it on the cake."

I look at our beautiful white cake that was supposed to have the traditional cake topper bride and groom. Barney was dressed in a suit and Barbie was dressed in a white dress.

All I can do is shake my head. I had no words. It was all funny and I couldn't be mad. Because, after all, it was now our tradition to outdo each other with our Elf on the Shelf shenanigans. This one certainly took the cake, and he knew it.

"You win," I whisper and kiss my husband.

Merry Elfing Christmas!

The End

www.ingramcontent.com/pod-product-compliance
Lightning Source LLC
Chambersburg PA
CBHW071322140726
47996CB00005B/1772